Beatles and Beacons

FRAN RAYA

The Book Guild Ltd

First published in Great Britain in 2024 by
The Book Guild Ltd
Unit E2 Airfield Business Park,
Harrison Road, Market Harborough,
Leicestershire. LE16 7UL
Tel: 0116 2792299
www.bookguild.co.uk
Email: info@bookguild.co.uk
Twitter: @bookguild

Typeset in 11pt Minion Pro

Printed and bound by CPI Group (UK) Ltd, Croydon, CR0 4YY

ISBN 978 1916668 058

British Library Cataloguing in Publication Data.
A catalogue record for this book is available from the British Library.

MIX
Paper | Supporting
responsible forestry
FSC® C013604

I wish to dedicate this book to the memory of John Lennon, George Harrison, and all the departed loved ones and friends that The Beatles were connected to.

Also in memory of my beloved husband, Rob, who I adored, and was always there at my side for forty-nine years. Our love will never die.

Once upon another time, about a million songs ago, there lived a musical group on a teenager's bedroom wall. These persons raided her Queendom on an ordinary October day, through her dad's Bakelite wireless. The song they sang was a tuneful newness and she helped it touch number seventeen in a memorable chart of yesterday, specifically 1962.

Take a trip throughout the 1960s through the eyes and mind of Rebecca Beacon, who is just twelve years old when she becomes aware of The Beatles, at the very beginning of their burgeoning fame.

Her teenage years are exciting but also saturated with angst and harsh realities, made bearable by her musical icons, as she retreats into a world of imagination. She perceives them as beacons of light, shining through the darkness, lifting her spirit, and touching her soul.

This semi-autobiographical story by Fran Raya will strike a nostalgic chord for fans of the same generation, but also for the many admirers of the band, who are too young to have witnessed Beatlemania in full flow. Nothing prepared the world for their emergence.

Rebecca Beacon finds her own identity as a result of her obsession, which proves to be both inspirational and turbulent in equal measure.

Chapter One

Rebecca Beacon, or Becca, as she preferred to be called, was sitting on the couch in her parents' front room. She was trying to block out the constant prattle of her two aunts, who were informing her mother about the new greengrocers that now stocked a plentiful supply of bananas. Their conversation was peppered with tittle-tattle and endless prattle about the comings and goings of the neighbours and their disorderly lives.

Gossiping behind each other's backs was a lifelong hobby, although her mother, Shirley, usually refrained from such inappropriate behaviour. She just listened in, and half-smiled, so that they would think she agreed. As for Becca, well, it was all so boring for a just-turned twelve-year-old in early October 1962. She considered herself to be somewhat cool, on the lines of her teenage brother, Mikey, who idolised James Dean.

Becca sighed and went into the lounge to switch on the wireless to hear the latest music. She sang along with Joe Brown's 'A Picture of You', which had featured largely in the charts that summer. It gave her a sense of freedom and she jumped around the room with her tennis racket as a substitute guitar. She applauded at the end of the record.

Then another song raided her Queendom. She had never heard it before, and it stopped her in her tracks. It was different. Simple but unique. *Who are they? I love this.* She listened intently, waiting for the name of the singers and felt a funny tingling sensation throughout her body. She heard the presenter say, "now that was an up-and-coming group from Liverpool called The Beatles with their debut single 'Love Me Do.'"

Beetles? She laughed out loud at the name, thinking it was spelt like the insects, but she was already hooked on their song. She could not wait to hear it again and lingered expectantly, with her ears glued to the broadcast, just in case. No such luck.

The next day she got ready for school. She wore her new uniform with pride, checking herself in the long mirror in her bedroom. She had recently won a place at a grammar school and was full of self-regard over the fact. She tilted her beret to one side, brushing her fringe away from her large, brown eyes. She preened and posed for a while until her father shouted up the stairs.

"Michael! Becca! You're both going to be late, and you've not had any breakfast!"

"Coming, Daddy," she replied, still admiring herself in the looking glass. She made her way to the table and wolfed down her porridge.

"Don't eat so fast," advised her father.

In the background the radio was playing away. She was just about to put on her blazer, when a familiar harmonica plundered the airways, and the hairs on the back of her shapely neck stood to instant attention. "Oh! Shh, everyone! I want to listen to this song!" She switched up the volume very high.

"Becca! What's wrong with you? And turn that thing down! Such a noise!" complained her mother.

"It's those Beetles!"

"Beetles? What a silly name."

"Just shush! I need to listen to them! Please!"

Her parents looked at each other, shaking their heads. Becca's fifteen-year-old brother, Michael, appeared out of nowhere, in time to hear the last verse.

"I'm late," he mumbled as he fought with his coat sleeves, grabbing a piece of toast and stuffing it into his mouth while he struggled to put on his school jacket. "Who's the group?"

"Oh, Mikey, have you ever heard anything like this before?" enthused Becca.

He stopped for a moment and his ears pricked up like a dog with powers of perception. "Who are they? They're good."

"The Beetles!" she exclaimed, still thinking they spelt their name that way.

"Wait a minute! A friend of a friend told me about them. They're quite a name in Liverpool and play at a rock club called… erm… The Tavern. No, I mean The Cavern."

"The Cavern? Daddy, can we go there the next time we see Uncle David and Aunty Rose?" requested Becca excitedly.

Becca and her father made regular trips to Liverpool to see his brother and sister-in-law. Before they visited them, they would travel on the ferry across the Mersey to New Brighton. Becca liked The Royal Daffodil the best. When they arrived, they always took the long walk up the promenade to Wallasey. Once there, they would sit on the sand, eating the egg and cress sandwiches that her father had prepared in advance. This whole routine was an integral part of her childhood to date.

"We'll talk about this later. For now, school. Both of you!" insisted their father.

They waved goodbye to their parents and rushed to the local railway station. Michael attended a different school, but in the same direction as Becca's. Normally he would not want to be seen with his little sister in tow, but this day was unusual. His curiosity had been aroused by Becca's enthusiasm for the so-called Beetles. He was music-mad and was learning to play the guitar in his spare time. He wore trendy sunglasses, even when it was raining. Becca felt good walking beside him.

"Mikey, can you ask your friend of a friend whether the Beetles are going to be on TV?"

"I'll find out anyway because I want to know myself."

Becca felt her heartbeat double, but she did not understand why. Maybe it was some kind of meaningful premonition or a magical intervention. She was very different to her friends and possessed a wild imagination, a hidden streak of devilry just waiting to be ignited. She had written numerous poems and short stories from a very early age. She could also sing and was in the school choir, not that she relished performing some of the dire songs they were given to warble. She was so disenchanted that sometimes she mimed them. Nobody ever knew.

She was twelve years peculiar and knew nothing much except acceptance. She attended a grammar school made of sad bricks and watered-down awareness. She half-listened to her elders, polished off her homework, flattered her examinations and complemented her prayers.

All that was true, until the historic date of the 17th October 1962. Mikey had found out that The Beatles – who Becca now knew was spelled with an 'a' – were going to appear on *People and Places,* a topical magazine programme, filmed at Granada TV Studios in Manchester. He was watching it with friends at another house. Her excitement was at fever pitch because, at last, she would be able to connect faces to their voices.

"What about your homework?" queried her mother.

Becca was sitting cross-legged on the floor about a yard away from the television screen.

"Not now. After this. I promise," she replied breathlessly.

"I don't know! All this fuss over a noisy group of deadbeats!"

"You don't understand!"

"Well at least we agree on that one."

"Oh, *please!* They're on in a few minutes."

"With a bit of luck, it'll put you off them for good! If I hear you sing 'Love Me Too' one more time, I'll scream."

"It's 'Love Me *Do*!"

"Too or do – it's all the same to me."

Becca remained pasted to the carpet. She looked up just in time, as the presenter introduced them. Her eyes widened and her mouth fell open. She felt as if she had been struck by lightning. The music seemed to fade into the background, because all she saw was four amazing creatures in matching made-to-measure suits, adorned with guitars and a drumkit. She felt herself being incredibly drawn to two of them. She stuck a fist into her mouth because her emotions were ridiculously off the scale. As they sang 'Some Other Guy' and then the much played 'Love Me Do', it was as if she was inside the television, standing next to them, watching from the side. She had this unbearable urge to invade their space and her imagination went into full overdrive.

Hello, my name's Becca Beacon, and I think your songs and voices are just fantastic. You're all so gorgeous and amazing. Which one are you? It's so good to meet you at last. Oh, you've stopped singing and now you're talking. Be quiet, Becca. Just listen.

Then she found out their names. The two she was inexplicably bewitched by were called John and Paul. The other guitarist was George and the drummer, Ringo. But they all shone, and she was breathless with her first real experience of strong physical attraction. She was so starstruck that she could not move and remained in the same position for a while.

"Well? Are you impressed?" asked her mother, with more than a touch of cynicism.

Becca heard her mum's voice winging its way across the room, but the words did not resonate.

"Are you going to sit there all night, or will we be having the pleasure of your company at the table for dinner?"

She turned her head round to face her, eyes glazed, and in a world of her own.

"Did you hear me, Becca?"

There was no reply. For the moment her mother looked concerned. She had never seen her daughter so stupefied. Her chatter-boxing had taken a sabbatical and was out for the count.

"Becca, talk to me. What's the matter? Don't tell me it's because of those four reprobates! I watched them and they're not a patch on the crooners. They can't even sing properly, and the lyrics are so bland. Becca! For heaven's sake, pull yourself together," she demanded.

"Mummy, I'm in love."

"Oh, give me strength. I've never heard such nonsense."

"No. I mean it. I love them. They're just wonderful."

*

From the second that their photographs adorned her bedroom walls, the changes moved in greedily. It was smack, bang, crash, and pandemonium. Things altered dramatically but not always for the best. Becca was utterly obsessed and became an aficionado of all things Beatles.

Her icons kept her warm throughout the Big Freeze of 1963. Bitterly cold temperatures, blizzards, and endless snow lasted from December 1962 right the way through until the following March. Thermometers plummeted, bringing endless chaos. But Becca was Beatle-insulated.

As the year progressed, she acquired Beatle books, photographs, newspaper articles and magazines. Then there were the utterly mind-blowing Beatle records. She drooled over Beatle jackets, Beatle suits, Beatle boots and Beatle haircuts. She begged her father, Eric, to buy her a

Beatle lampshade, which he did against her mother's wishes. She had pain in her jaw from chewing Beatle bubblegum, because each purchase included a small photograph of them and she needed every single one to fill the special album provided. Often, she would find a duplicate copy of a picture that she already possessed, so she swapped it with other Beatle fanatics for one that was missing from her collection.

She tuned in to Beatle broadcasts and squealed at every Beatle TV appearance. More significantly, she joined the all-important Beatles Fanclub. There was only one word to describe it, that became synonymous with their surreal domination: Beatlemania. Where was she in all this frenzy? Trapped inside a Beatle sandwich of juicy John, pickled Paul, cheddared George and relished Ringo. It was no joke. Especially when she was surrounded by stern faces and twisted mouths telling her that she was half-doped. Her age was a problem to the problem.

Suddenly, the convivial girl became the general nuisance. Speedily, the teacher's pet became his newly born nightmare. Frighteningly, the academic mind was invaded by a musical intensity. Unbearably, the girl became aware of sexual magnetism. Anonymously, she emblazoned her frenzied adoration on every chalkable object. Ridiculously, her whole maidenhood somersaulted in a Merseyside melodrama that exhausted her lifestyle and unsettled her parents.

*

The autumn of 1963 was spent on bicycles, often cycling to Granada TV Studios with her friends in the crazy hope of sighting the Fab Four, as they were called. There was always the faint possibility they could be lurking within the sheltered corridors of that tantalizing structure.

Her thirteenth birthday fell two weeks before their *Sunday Night at The London Palladium* debut appearance. The day after the show, the whole school buzzed with a heightened sense of their televised impact. The staff would make mention of their performance in the lessons, and she would cringe visibly at their interest because it reeked of hypocrisy. Somehow, teachers and Beatles were sour milk. They interrogated her in the hope of dispelling her seemingly senseless obsession. They wrote acid reports to mark the end of each term. They tried to brainwash her with theories that belonged to a pointless past. They attempted to drown her in a vat of useless information. They wanted to suffocate her under a sheet of false realisation. They loved to strangle her with a string of worn-out virtuosos. They confiscated her poems and sketches and wished to rob her of the only important part of her adolescence. But they failed. Spectacularly!

If the world was driving her mad with monotony, irony or angst, *they* were always there like four beacons of light, banishing the darkest stormy clouds, and lifting her dreamlike reality onto higher planes. Her elders did not understand why she insisted on clutching at this shooting star, or why she wanted to wrap the four of them in cotton wool, place them in her cabinet and dust them down with unbridled inspiration.

Back home, the atmosphere was electric with a twin fever. Apart from the times spent with her friends at their houses, listening to the familiar hit sounds of the early 1960s, the real magic was always captured within the privacy of her bedroom walls. Only then would it become the intense phenomenon in full dramatic flow. She would fix her gaze on their photographs that were plastered all over the four walls. The pictures around her were no longer inanimate. Each face, each smile, each wink was vibrantly alive. Each mouth addressed her worshiping ears. Each hand reached out to touch her own. Each foot thumped out that unmistakable rhythm. Each musical instrument pulsated, twanged, and vibrated. Her bed became the stage. The floor morphed into the stalls. The mirror changed into a camera. The lampshade was a blinding spotlight. The music blasted out of her overworked record player and invaded the whole room. The air was saturated with melodies, soft and loud, slow and fast, hard and long. Around her she had it all. Here lay her Queendom. The Beatles were singing for her. The Beatles were creating for her. The Beatles were joking with her. The Beatles were living for her. The Beatles were discovered for one crucial benefit: herself!

She had power at her fingertips and stood unique and fixated inside a teenage fantasia. She was impregnable. She belonged. Her throat was alight as she sang out the words to each song, watching herself in the dressing table mirror. Her body was drained as she flung herself into different directions and shapes to match the music. Their music. Their influence. Her gain. Laughing with John. Singing with Paul. Walking with George. Dancing with Ringo. She was a Beatle extension, a part of the legend, a link in an everlasting historical chain. Their friends became hers. Their joy was her joy. Their lives were her life. It was like a spiritual interconnection of something extraordinary.

She knew they would become everything they strove to be and reach the absolute pinnacle of fame. As they drove that stallion to the heights of the dazzling rainbow, she was too young to understand that they were just a human revelation. She was too naïve to put the whole jigsaw into perspective; far too hung up with adolescent lectures to realise that they were there to be greatly appreciated and not worshipped. That is where Becca fell, but she was trapped inside a creative cage of her own making, and she could not escape.

"What's happened to you, Becca?" asked her mother in an almost desperate tone. "You used to be such a good girl. Your head's crammed full of those… those four long-haired louts. It's ridiculous and quite alarming."

She blew an enormous gumball with her mouth from the never-ending supply bought every day in the hope of completing her Beatle bubblegum album. After several weeks of jaw ache, she needed just one more photograph to complete the set. But it was like looking for gold dust. *Number sixteen is avoiding me. I've got to find it. Keep chewing.*

"I'm talking to you."

"Sorry, Mum, but I'm busy."

"Doing what exactly?"

"Looking for number sixteen."

"You're not making any sense and stop chewing gum. Night and day you're blowing bubbles."

"Because I need card number sixteen, and until I get it there'll be loads of chewing and lots more bubbles."

"Card number sixteen? Oh, don't tell me it's the four mopheads again! I might have known. For heaven's sake."

"You just don't get it."

"And you don't understand that if you neglect your studies and get more detentions, your father and I will be summoned again by your headmistress. It was hard enough the last time. I've never been so embarrassed."

"Don't be. She's a drag. She thinks she's Queen Elizabeth and she's forever picking on me. She's dead grotty and she's always got her nose in the air."

"Grotty?"

"Grotesque."

"So now you're talking slang. I wonder where you learnt that from? Ah, let me guess. The four degenerates. This is becoming ludicrous now. They've taken you over. I don't recognise you anymore."

"They're fab. Everyone knows it except you."

"I watched that John Lemon in an interview the other night. He's rude and arrogant."

"His name's John *Lennon,* not Lemon! He's sexy and cool."

"And the other one, Paul McCarthy, just seems to laugh at everything he does or says."

"It's Paul *McCartney!* He's absolutely gorgeous and very close to John. They write all their incredible songs together."

Shirley Beacon frowned. She was from a generation of women who had weathered World War Two and lived by a code of conventional ethics. She worked part-time as a dressmaker, but she could also sing and had a deep, bluesy voice that was so powerful she did not need a microphone. She was pretty and warm-hearted with green eyes. She adored 'Swing' and her favourite crooner was Dean

Martin. Her husband, Eric, was a bookkeeper for a clothing company, but he'd played piano in a jazz band for fun, so they knew all about the love of music. Shirley was one of four sisters. She was particularly close to her youngest sibling, Mary. They were nearest in age and fashioned out of the same long-established egg. Family, duty, and respectability. In that order. They were still known as the Allens – her maiden name, before she became a Beacon. Inwardly, she thought the surname Beacon was rather bizarre, but she loved her husband unreservedly, so she kept that opinion to herself. He came from a long line of Beacons and was very proud of his heritage, so she would not dream of upsetting the ancestral apple cart. Besides, she had a decent life and counted her many blessings. However, this never-ending infuriating performance from her daughter set her teeth on edge and flew in the face of everything she held dear.

Her thoughts were interrupted abruptly by Becca screeching so loudly that her ears vibrated.

"I've got it! I've got it! Number sixteen! Now I've the *whole* set! This is the best day of my life!" Becca jumped off the couch and began to dance around the room singing 'She Loves You' at the top of her tuneful voice.

Shirley was speechless as she watched her daughter in full Beatle-flight. *She's lost the plot! You'd think she'd won the football pools. I've never seen such a hysterical reaction over a picture album of four roughnecks. Oh, my word!*

"Mum, what did you do with my Beatle jacket? I want to wear it today."

Becca's jacket had been custom-made by her aunty Doris, who was a top-class seamstress. She had given her a photograph of her idols in their Pierre Cardin-style suits, and Doris had created the collarless design, just for Becca. She wore it with her school shirt and tie, teamed with jeans. Her hair was cut in Beatle fashion, her fringe practically covering her large brown eyes.

"I gave it away," lied Shirley.

"What!"

"I donated it to charity."

"What!"

"You heard me."

"No! Tell me it's not true!" exclaimed Becca on the verge of a major tantrum.

"Stop it! All right, I didn't, but your reaction speaks volumes. Why are you so obsessed? They're only human, or at least I think they are. The world's gone mad."

Becca controlled herself but felt very angry. She berated her mother for her lack of understanding.

"Why make up a thing like that? You know I love that jacket. Anyway, Aunty Doris made it especially for me. She gets it! So do Dad and Mikey. It's *you* who won't give them a chance. Have you really listened to their music? I don't mean just the singles. Their LP is so amazing. It includes quite a few of their own songs. They send me."

"They send me, too. Usually out of the room."

"Oh, poo! I can't talk to you anymore."

"When you start concentrating on your studies and stop entertaining the classroom with your crackpot antics, then I might listen. Might! Your last school report was a disgrace. Your form master was scathing in his remarks!"

"That's his opinion. I still do my best."

"Your best? You call four detentions in three months your best? I'd hate to see you at your worst."

"The rules are just daft. I get a detention for not fastening my tie properly, or not wearing my stupid hat, or running down the endless corridors. I'm good at English, art and music. They should encourage me, not spend all their time pointing fingers and confiscating my Beatle magazines."

"According to your exasperated English teacher, you were secretly reading the mopheads monthly, instead of *The History of Mr. Polly.* Beatle books are not part of the syllabus. What do you expect him to do? Reward you? Of course he confiscated it, because it's unacceptable."

"He needs to give it me back."

"You need to show him some respect."

"He needs to dig it!"

Shirley raised her hazel eyes to the ceiling. More juvenile slang. It was like talking to the rebellious wall.

"I truly hope that this madness will pass. You're at a very funny age and open to all kinds of outside influences. For my own peace of mind, I'd like to think that this is a temporary crush."

"Well, it isn't! Now here's a huge surprise for you: the beloved Beatles have been asked to appear on *The Royal Command Performance.* So, what do you think of that, eh? You looked shocked," smirked Becca at her mother's disbelief.

"*The Royal Command Performance!* You mean they're going to inflict their caterwauling on the royal family and the unsuspecting public at large! I can't believe it!"

"Their songs are fantastic and now the whole of England will realise that they're here to stay."

Shirley was lost in thought. *All I can hear is yeah, yeah, yeah. What kind of lyric is that? Not to mention the constant shaking of their heads, while they ooh and aah, and the audience goes hysterical. Girls screaming and fainting, boys shouting and waving. The police must cordon off the area wherever the group goes, because someone will get crushed or trampled underfoot. The law has much better things to see to than protecting a herd of uncontrollable teenagers. It's a disease that's spreading at a frightening pace, but there's no vaccine and my wilful daughter is at the forefront of it all.*

"I'm going round to see Aunty Jean. I've baked her a cake for her birthday. We've all been invited to her party tomorrow," said Shirley, changing the subject completely.

Becca's playful mood evaporated instantly. She hated visiting her mother's best friend and she had good reason to feel that way.

"I don't want to go."

"Why?"

"I just don't."

"This will be the second time you've refused an invitation. I suppose you want to play your Beatle records at full blast while we're out of the house!"

"She's not my aunty."

"No, but you've called her that since you were a little girl, out of respect."

"I still don't want to go."

"Explain."

"I can't."

"There must be a reason. Is it because of Larry? I know he can be a bit playful at times but he's her only son and you've been friends since you were babies."

"It's nothing to do with Larry."

"Then what?"

"I don't like… I don't like his dad."

"Uncle Ted?"

"He's not my uncle and he'll never be my uncle."

"What's he done?"

Becca looked at the floor and just shook her head.

"You can't come out with a statement like that and not explain properly."

"I don't want to talk about it. I just don't like him."

"Why not? He's been really good to you and Mikey. Especially you! Only last month he bought you a Beatle magazine and glossy photographs."

"He's creepy."

"In what way?"

"Oh, I don't know. He just is."

Shirley felt a frisson of alarm as she noted Becca's uncomfortable stance. Her gaze was firmly aimed at the floor, and she could not look her mother in the eye as she spoke.

"Anyway, I think I've got a cold coming on," she fibbed.

"Hmm. I've not heard you sneeze or cough."

"I've got a sore throat."

"How come it's just happened now when I told you about the birthday party?"

"It started this morning."

"Hmm."

"I'm going to do some homework, you'll be pleased to know."

Becca swiftly left the room and ran upstairs. Her heart was beating very fast and she felt sick.

She entered her bedroom and closed the door. The Beatles photographs and posters were plastered all over the walls. She spoke to them in a whisper, so nobody could hear.

"What should I do, John? Please tell me what to do. I can't tell anyone because *he* told me I'd be punished, and nobody would believe me anyway. What do you think, Paul?"

Becca sat on the bed and began to cry. The situation was becoming unbearable. Since the age of nine, 'uncle' Ted had been abusing her on a regular basis. It started when she was splashing around in Larry's rubber dinghy one summer. She had worn a pink-ruffled swimming costume and looked cute. Suddenly, a large pair of hands rested on her chest and stayed there. She froze as she had looked round to see Ted, misty-eyed, and breathing heavily as he whispered into her ear.

"You're such a pretty little thing. Do you know that, Becca? Do you know how you make me feel? You're very wet. Why don't you come into the house and dry yourself. I'll help you. Let me help you."

She had pulled away from him and found shelter behind Larry, who was totally oblivious to his father's perversion.

"Hey, Becca Beacon, let's play cricket in the street. We can use the gatepost as a wicket. What d'ya say?" suggested Larry, with a wide grin, much to her relief. Becca loved sport, so she had fallen in with his request. She was only too glad to be away from Ted and his wandering hands.

This had set a pattern over the last three years. Ted propositioned her whenever, or wherever, he could, with smutty words and disgusting physical gestures. Her mother was very close with Larry's whole family, which made the whole thing even more unbearable. Becca wanted to confide in her parents about the appalling situation, but Ted had brainwashed her into thinking it was *all* her fault anyway. He made her feel dirty and ashamed.

The tears rolled down her cheeks. Ted's 'dictum' kept going round and round in her troubled head, like a record stuck on its turntable.

"Pretty little Becca. Now remember, this is our secret, and, if you tell, I'll make sure that everyone knows that it was all *your* idea. Your mum will be so angry, and your dad will smack you hard. They'll all see that you're a very naughty girl and nobody will want to be with you. *You'll* be the one with a bad name. Not me. So just come here and let me touch you. Yes?"

She had mumbled a lame excuse and ran away. She heard his repulsive laughter as she'd fled down the street, her heart thumping inside her ribcage. She was far too disturbed to go home, so she'd scarpered to the end of the road and climbed through the railings which led onto open fields. She made sure to keep away from the reservoir because the bottom of Ted's back garden was a short cut to that section. So, she'd darted the other way towards the hilly landscape that provided a route to the local dyeworks.

Why doesn't he leave me alone? I hate him. He's a dirty old man. I wish he was dead.

She came back into the present, and when she stopped crying she needed her usual musical fix. She hugged the 'Please Please Me' LP cover and reverently took out the large vinyl disc. She placed it very carefully on the turntable of her faithful record player, and waited for the first track, 'I Saw Her Standing There', to begin. The second she heard Paul's voice, she was lost. All prior dread and fear were blasted away as she plunged into her make-believe world. Ted's revolting advances were replaced by her developing, hot-blooded feelings for both John and Paul, her body tingling all over with a passion that she did not fully understand. It was the antithesis of her revulsion with regards to her abuser.

She had to cleanse herself of inflicted shame, and by feeling an intense and barely controllable emotion for her two fantasy heartthrobs, it erased all the filth and repugnance of Ted's unforgivable actions. It would also leave her free to embrace physical contact with boyfriends in the future, without feeling nauseous. She switched up the volume and heard the familiar knocking sound under the floor. It was her mother, banging on the sitting room ceiling with a sweeping brush handle as a mark of protest to turn the sound down. When 'Twist and Shout' came on, Becca increased the amplification even more, partly to annoy her mother, but mostly to worship John's leather tonsils in full Lennon-flow. In her head she could visualise him performing the song with his guitar held high, legs slightly apart, bending his knees to the rhythm of the beat.

No wonder I've got to scream! It's too much! He's too much! It shouldn't be allowed. Oh, my goodness.

She began to sing and dance on her bed, kissing their photographs on the wall. In the middle of her obsessive reverie, the door opened. It was her mother with a face like a farmer's wife's backside on a frosty morning.

"Becca, for God's sake! Turn that unbearable noise down, or, better still, switch it off!"

"No!"

"What happened to your sore throat? You sound like a wildcat! I can't keep up with your moods!" shouted Shirley at the top of her voice in order to be heard above the music.

"What happened to the mum I love? You used to be such fun!"

Shirley, in a fit of sheer frustration, grabbed the tonearm of the gramophone and yanked it across the record, scratching the vinyl with the stylus, and damaging it in the process.

"Look what you've done! You've ruined it! How could you?"

"It was an accident."

"I hate you and I hate school! You're all the same! Telling me what to do, how to dress, how to behave! I want to be *me*. You want me to be 'little miss twinset' with matching pearls!"

"No, Becca. I just want my daughter back! I don't know who you are! The Beatles have corrupted you. Just look at you! Fringe halfway down your face, panstick on your lips, black polo neck jumper with skin-tight jeans. I can't remember the last time I saw your legs!"

"You see them every day of the week when I wear that grotty gymslip for the lessons with the teachers from hell."

Shirley took a deep breath. She remembered when Becca had passed her scholarship and how proud she was to wear the uniform. But that was pre-Beatles and another world away.

"Where do we go from here? I truly don't know what to do."

"How about buying me another 'Please Please Me' LP to replace the one you just scratched to death? If you don't, I know for sure that Dad will. In the meantime, I'll borrow Mikey's. You don't get at him when he plays his Beatle records."

"I don't like his taste in music but at least he doesn't play the blasted songs so loud!"

"Loud enough."

Shirley sat down on the bed. She felt lightheaded and stressed. She'd had a problem with a supervisor on the factory floor beforehand. He was very belligerent, and she had to call the manager for help. She'd felt threatened and vulnerable by his bullying tactics. She did not like confrontation, especially in the workplace. She could not handle her daughter's rebellious outbursts. The more she tried to talk sense into her way of thinking, the worse the predicament became.

Becca's father had a much better relationship with her and handled her obsession in an understanding way. He had a very dry wit and made Becca laugh on a continual basis. She had inherited his sense of the farcical. Laughter was the best medicine in the world.

Her dad and brother were Manchester City supporters, and Becca would tag along with them to Maine Road and watch their team play football. She had been attending matches since the late-1950s and looked forward to the whole experience. It was a bit like a see-saw syndrome. City would perform well one season, but they'd concede too many points, and relegation beckoned the next year. But she still stayed loyal. Once a blue, always a blue.

Her mother had shaken her head when Becca's dad bought her the full Manchester City regalia. Scarf, bobble hat, rattle and all the programmes. Becca was very good at the rudiments of the game and also knew all the players' names. She was infatuated with the sport, but this was nowhere near the obsession she now had for The Beatles.

"I thought she was going over the top about Manchester City, but that pales into insignificance compared to the so-called Fab Four. She's well and truly brainwashed. It's like she's possessed or something. Have you seen her when she watches them on TV? Squirming on the floor and screaming her head off at the close ups of John and Paul. It's not normal."

"Oh, Shirley, it's just her age," Eric would say with a smile. "She's not on her own. There are thousands of girls all over the country who feel the same way about The Beatles. It's all part of growing up and going through the stages of their teenage years. She'll change her mind eventually. In the meantime, buying their records and merchandise, well, what's the harm? If it makes her happy, then so be it. She'll soon settle down at school as she gets older."

Back in the present, Shirley remembered his words. She saw the defiance on Becca's face, her eyes full of anger and rebellion as she swept her fringe away.

"All I'm telling you is to turn that bloody noise down. Is that too much to ask?"

"I'm going round to Aunty Mary's. She's easier to talk to and really gets me! Don't bother making me anything. I'll have to eat with her," replied Becca, completely ignoring her mother's request.

“Not everyone loves The Beatles’ music, Becca. It’s brash and I don’t rate them.”

Becca just stormed out of the room There was nothing more to say. Only time would tell.

Chapter Two

On the 4th October 1963, Becca's icons appeared on *Ready Steady Go.* Then on the 4th November they shone on *The Royal Command Performance,* and if that was not enough to send her reeling, their second LP 'With The Beatles' was released on the 22nd of the same month. It coincided with the horrendous assassination of John F. Kennedy in Dallas, Texas. As tragic and traumatic as that event was, Becca was still utterly fixated and focused on The Beatles and their incredible songs and looks. They dominated the music charts and had the whole country under their spell.

Her brother Mikey had just celebrated his sixteenth birthday and looked like a Beatle extension. He had mastered the guitar and had formed a group with some school friends. They played at local venues and parties and were very popular. It was Becca who had thought of their name.

"I know! Why don't you go as The Beacons?" she'd raved.

The Beacons attracted followers, even before anybody had heard them play, simply by the name.

"Hey Mikey," a fan had gushed, "your band is so cool. I love the way you sing Beatles songs. Can you play 'All My Loving'?"

"Yeah, we'll do that one next," he'd replied, eyes hidden behind the ever-present sunglasses.

Becca had very mixed emotions. On one hand she was ecstatic that The Beatles had infiltrated the very fabric of musical invention and were now lauded for their wonderful compositions. On the contrary, she was ridiculously resentful that she had to share them with everybody else. *I was one of the first to find them! All my school friends had never even heard of them! I had Beatle pics stuck to the inside lid of my desk in 1962! Even the teachers missed that one! Ha! Nobody knew who they were! And now everybody wants to be in on the action! They're mine! Go away!*

At home the atmosphere was rather turbulent. Her mother was still on her anti-Beatles soapbox and her father had lost his job. He had become rather withdrawn, especially when he could not find new employment.

"Honestly Shirley, I'm sick and tired of searching. All I want is to work again. I hate being unemployed and short of money. It's degrading," he grumbled.

"Something will come along, Eric. Please don't lose heart. Now, why don't you sign on the dole? You've paid National Insurance contributions, so you're entitled to the help," she coaxed gently.

"I won't accept charity! I've worked all my life and I'm not going anywhere with a bloody begging bowl."

"Oh, Eric, it's not charity and we need the money."

"Don't you think I know that?" he groaned, scratching his head.

"Look, there's no shame in getting help temporarily. You've earnt it. I'm really worried because Mikey and Becca will need new clothes and shoes, especially their school uniforms, and that can be expensive."

"Rub it in, why don't you?"

"I'm just talking sense. We must look at practical issues. There's not enough money in the kitty."

"Oh really? What about the five pound note that your sister, Mary, leaves behind the clock every week? I'm not daft, I know she feels sorry for you. I mean, her husband's well-settled. A surveyor no less. Personally, I can't stand him. And I've seen the expression on both of their faces when they talk about their opulent lifestyle. They think they're above everybody else!"

Shirley bit her lip before she replied. There was an element of truth to his words regarding her sister's husband, Don, but Eric was wrong about Mary. She may look contented on the surface, but Shirley knew the real story about her 'ideal' marriage. Don was a womaniser and Mary was deeply unhappy about the whole situation. Their only daughter, Lisa, had just celebrated her twelfth birthday, and they'd thrown a lavish party for her. Mary was not short of cash but bereft of marital fidelity. Shirley took a deep breath before she spoke.

"I didn't want to hurt you, so I decided not to tell you about the five pound note. Mary does it with a good heart, not to humiliate you, or feel sorry for me."

"Then why hide it from me?"

"Because she knows you're proud. She also knows that you're a wonderful husband, unlike Don."

"Unlike Don? What do you mean?"

"I've never told you this but maybe I should have done. Our situation isn't permanent because I'm sure you'll get another job. Mary's circumstances are appalling."

Eric frowned. His curiosity superseded any grudges.

"Just explain," he requested, looking at Shirley with concern when he saw her troubled face.

"Don's having an affair. One of many it seems. Mary's a very attractive, but unhappy, wife, still in love with her husband."

"I had no idea. Poor Mary. I always thought that Don was a selfish sod. Does he know that she knows?"

"No. She's afraid he'll walk out, into the arms of his latest flame."

"He needs a wake-up call. He's an apology for a human being. Poor Mary. I thought she was like him, but she's been putting on an act all the time."

"She's scared of him. He's raised his hands more than once to her."

"He's *what?* So, he's a wife-beater as well as a philanderer! Shirley, why haven't you told me all this before?"

"Mary doesn't want the family to know."

Eric shook his head with disbelief. His deep-set brown eyes looked darker with projected anger and his handsome face creased up into a twisted expression. His hands clenched into fists as though he was getting ready for a physical fight. He was not a violent man, but he felt an overpowering urge to punch Don on his snooty nose.

"He's a rotten, stinking swine! You don't know how close I am to going round there and giving him what for! I've always disliked him, but now, I detest him! He's scum!"

"I know. I agree with you, but I've vowed to keep this a secret. I can't break that promise. It's been hard for me, too. I really want to confide in Doris and Doreen, but where do I start? Do you remember the last time Mary and Don came to dinner? She wore a beautiful turquoise chiffon scarf that she wouldn't take off? Well, she showed me the bruises around her neck where he'd grabbed her. Quite honestly, I feel like going round to the police, let alone social services."

"Well, I think we should! What if something terrible happens to her? And there's Lisa. This is bound to affect your niece. Surely your sisters will step in before it gets completely out of hand?"

"I'm trying to convince Mary to report him, but she won't budge. I'm worried sick for her welfare and sanity."

Eric sighed deeply. Everything was upside down in his life. No job, no money, and now his sister-in-law was at the mercy of her violent, unfaithful husband. On top of all that, Becca was constantly rebelling against her mother's advice and was abusing good schooling for the sake of her endless obsession with all-things Beatles. Although he defended her most of the time, inwardly he could see the writing on the educational wall if she did not knuckle down to her book learning.

Maybe Shirley's right and I should be discouraging her away from her musical fantasy. Becca told me that she wants to write songs and sing when she leaves school. That's taking this mania a step too far. Mind you, Shirley used to sing semi-professionally and can still hold a good tune. I played piano in a jazz band as a hobby, but it was such fun. I remember strumming the banjo as well. We busked on a ship going over to Ireland and put a hat on the floor in front of us, just for a joke. It was overflowing with silver and copper! We didn't expect that reaction. So, we kept the money! Why not? Golden memories of happy, carefree times before the children came along. Mikey's rebellious but controllable. Our Becca? She's a different kettle of frantic fish.

Shirley interrupted his thoughts.

"I think I will speak to Doris and Doreen. I know I promised Mary I wouldn't, but quite frankly it's just a very hard secret to keep. We've got enough going on under our own roof at the moment, without this additional problem. I've always had a huge soft spot for Mary, but I'm going to confide in my other sisters. I think that Doreen, especially, will know what to do. She's outspoken but very down to earth and good at sorting out situations."

"I agree. Mary needs all the help she can get. She'll thank us in the end."

"Hopefully."

Eric nodded and walked to the cloakroom to get his coat.

"Where are you going?" puzzled Shirley.

"To the Labour Exchange to look for a job. I'll sign on the dole until something comes up."

"What made you change your mind?"

"Mary. It puts everything else into perspective."

Shirley felt her eyes prick with unshed tears. A solitary teardrop trickled down her cheek and Eric kissed it away.

When he left, she put on her apron and peeled some potatoes and carrots to go with the stewing steak she had bought for their evening meal. She was deep in thought and wished that her mother was still alive. She had passed away when Shirley was only sixteen, leaving her father, Jack, to shoulder the burden of four daughters. Her older sisters, Doris and Doreen, were single and living together, along with their father, who was now in his late seventies and unwell. Doreen had stopped working so she could look after him full time. She was a wonderful cook and baker and practically lived in the kitchen.

Becca called round regularly to see them, especially her aunty Doris, who thought the world of her. She loved hearing about all her adventures, including her Beatles fixation. In fact, she looked forward to her visits tremendously as she embraced Becca's crazy antics and sense of fun. Doreen, on the other hand, thought Becca was completely over the top and unmanageable.

"You're a real Sarah Bernhardt, aren't you?" mocked Doreen, comparing her disparagingly to the famous French actress after listening to Becca's aspirations to be on the stage when she left school.

"No, Aunty Doreen. I want to write songs and sing them. Mind you, Sarah Bernhardt was one of a kind, so I guess it's not a bad comparison, is it?" replied Becca, double-crossing her eyes.

Doris stifled a giggle as Doreen pulled a face and disappeared into the kitchen, her well-ordered home ground. Becca just grinned and did a John Lennon daft dance across the carpet.

"Oh, Becca. You do make me laugh. But I must tell you that your mum's really worried about your schooling. We were all so proud of you when you passed your Eleven Plus and achieved your scholarship. Don't throw this golden opportunity away."

"It's a king-size drag. They teach you stuff you don't really need to know. Even when I get good marks, they still criticise my behaviour. The choirmaster, Mr. Brooks, whacked me round the head with some sheet music last week."

"Why?"

"Well, I told him that I prefer Lennon and McCartney to Edward Elgar, and reminded him that The Beatles do a great version of 'Roll Over Beethoven.'"

"Oh, Becca. What am I going to do with you? It's all very well joking outside of school, but try to buckle down a little. For me? I'm so proud of you. You're the daughter I never had."

"I know, Aunty Doris, but I just don't fit in. I'm different and have my own ideas on things. I'm dead serious about writing songs and singing them. I write parodies for the end of term concerts. Mostly about school rules. They always go down well with the pupils, but the teachers sit in a line, stony-faced and tight-lipped as if I've committed a crime."

"Parodies? You never told me."

"Well, I have now."

"Will you sing me one of them?"

"Of course. It's to the tune of 'The Mexican Hat Dance'.

It goes like this."

She cleared her throat, took a sip of lemonade, and sang in classic, Becca-mode:

"Oh, the teachers all give us the warning
To be bright and alert in the morning
It's God help us if we all start yawning
So we better sit up and be good.
There is English with our form master,
We should know it or there'll be disaster
We'll all end up in paris of plaster
So we better sit up and be good.
There are nouns and adverbial clauses
Which he skips through like the alphabet
He just reads on and he never pauses
As he thinks 'I shall teach them all yet'
So keep still, try until,
He stops giving you looks
Then read on with your books
And pretend that you don't
Feel so ill
From getting told off there's prevention
If you all sit up straight with attention
Or you'll find yourself stuck in detention
So you better sit up and be good
He might use an old axe or a hammer
And come down on you with such a whammer
If you don't sit and learn all your grammar
So you better sit up and be good
Just learn parts of speech without talking
Don't laugh or don't smile or don't scoff
If you do then you'll find yourself walking

To the headmistress to be told off
So beware, so take care
Or then he'll start to shout
And he'll pull you right out
To the front of the class
By your hair
Being good I should think you will try it
Without making a din or a riot
And you certainly all will be quiet
And all of you will
All of you will
All of you'll sit and be good."

Becca took a bow and her aunty clapped regardless of her former lecture.

"You've written that? You're only thirteen!"

"Not bad huh? I sing and write all the time. The Beatles have opened my eyes and ears to an even bigger planet of imagination. I was there before, but they've taken me by my hand and have showed me exactly the way to go forward. They're magical. Just magical."

"Why are they magical? They just stand and sit there, playing their guitars and drums. Their songs are all very similar. Tuneful, mind you, but nothing that special."

"Oh, Aunty Doris you're so wrong! Do you know they can't even read music? I mean, to create such melodies is little more than a miracle. And the way they look! I'm in love with John and Paul, especially. I can't explain it. They send me to another time and space. My whole body shakes. And they're so funny! I love it when the whole group's interviewed. It's that Liverpool wit."

"By this time next year, they might just fade away. It's hysteria at its height. These things don't last."

"Wrong again! They're going to America soon. After that, they'll conquer the world. I just know it."

"The world? Becca, the world is a huge place."

"They'll turn it on its head. Country by country. I think there's so much more to come. John and Paul will write new songs. I feel it strongly. It's only the beginning of their time."

"You really are obsessed. Your mum's right on that score. She takes it seriously, but I think you'll grow out of it all. There'll be other fads or hobbies."

"Maybe. But no other group will ever come close. Did you see them on *Late Scene Extra* and *Scene at 6.30* recently?"

"Can't say that I did."

"Well, they performed their latest single 'I Wanna Hold Your Hand'. The B-side is 'This Boy' and they sing it in three-part harmony. They mimed for some reason, but it still blew me away. Then Gay Byrne interviewed them with Ken Dodd. He's hilarious! I laughed my socks off at that one-off special. Such fun. They've got it all, Aunty Doris. Talent, looks, fashion and comedy. Just up my street. The four of them are fab, fab, fab and fab."

Doris looked at Becca's animated face as she praised her icons. She could see that her niece was enchanted beyond the normal level of admiration. But she knew that Becca was special, too. There was something about her that was completely different. Doris had read all her poems and little stories which she had penned as a child. They were very inventive.

When Becca had won the composition prize on Speech Day in 1961, at junior school, it was a proud moment. Doris remembered her going on the stage to collect her award – *Gulliver's Travels* by Jonathan Swift. Becca then read it at home, at least ten times, because it stretched her ideation even more. It was a highly competitive trophy and some of the other pupils in her year were resentful. Their essays may have been well written, but they lacked originality and that was the key to winning this prestigious prize. Imagination! Becca had that in spades.

"I believe that Mikey sings in a group with some school friends," acknowledged Doris. "Are they good?"

"They're really cool. I thought of their name."

"What is it?"

"The Beacons."

"I might have known." Doris laughed out loud. "Sounds like The Beatles but it's your family name. That's clever, Becca."

"My gifts are limitless," she boasted, fluttering her eyelashes repeatedly. "Just call me a genius. I don't mind."

"You know, I should really scold you, but I can't. You're a one-off, and I love you very much."

"Why thank you, Aunty Doris. Love you back. I'm just popping upstairs to see Grandpa before I leave. I desperately need to go home and hear John sing 'Not a Second Time'. It's a track on their latest LP. I absolutely love his voice. My legs go weak."

"Weak legs or not, your grandfather is very tired today, so don't overdo it with him. Be quiet and no hanky-panky."

"Or even hanky-pranky."

"That too."

Becca ran upstairs with heavy footsteps, and her aunty Doreen came out of the kitchen to investigate the noise.

"Is that Becca galloping up the stairs again?" she griped.

"Yes, she's just gone to see Dad."

"Did you tell her that he's not having such a good day? The last thing he needs to hear is another story about those blasted Beatles."

"She'll probably just talk about general things. Her friends possibly, and school."

"School! That's a joke! According to our Shirley, she's abusing her education and is a cheeky little madam. Her head's full of silly notions. She'll get nowhere with that attitude. Discipline is what she needs. Hard work and discipline. She should have lived through the war. That would have brought her back down to earth with a bang. I wish I would have had the same opportunities."

"Becca has a talent for writing. It's quite remarkable."

"In what way?"

"Her parodies, for a start."

"Parodies? She should be concentrating on studies. What use are parodies in the real world?"

"Doreen, the girl's only just thirteen. She's still finding her way."

"Lost her bloody way, you mean."

"No. She's a thinker with a vivid imagination."

"Well then, tell her to imagine good exam results. She nearly got expelled! Don't you remember? She broke into the gym one Sunday with her friend. They climbed through an open window. They didn't reckon on a teacher being in the building that day. He didn't believe they were pupils and called the law. They came home in a police car! Every curtain twitched in the street and what did Becca do? She skipped up the path singing a Beatle song! Our Shirley was mortified!"

"I know, I know. They both didn't fully understand the enormity of their actions. They just did it for a lark. They hadn't a clue that it was breaking and entering. It was very wrong, and Becca paid the price. Her spending money was stopped, and she was grounded for a month. She got the strap. Her headmistress thought it a fitting punishment. Personally, I think it's barbaric."

"Well, I don't, and anyway, it's not helped. She's still wild and rebellious."

"Not really. She's a good girl underneath. There's no harm in her, just teenage rebellion. She'll grow out of it all. You'll see."

"I doubt it. Have you seen that determined chin?"

"Oh, Doreen. You're not helping her with these remarks. She'll just kick against them all the more. Love and understanding is the answer. She's got a good heart, and one day all her dreams and aspirations will flourish. I just know it. Don't ask me why. It's a feeling."

"You and your feelings. No wonder you suffer with migraines. Becca's enough to give anyone a headache. You'll be getting the vinegar rags out soon and wrapping them round your head. Personally, I can't see how they help, and they stink the room out. I've got to open the windows wide, even on the coldest days."

Becca came racing down the stairs at that moment and said goodbye to both aunts, blowing kisses as she left. Doris blew some back, but Doreen just scowled and ambled once more into the kitchen to fry some fish and contemplate. *She's a first-class St. Trinian. I wish all her teachers the best of luck. They'll bloody well need it!*

*

Becca skipped along the pavement, skimming the weeds that were growing through the cracks. She felt good after talking to her aunty Doris, who always encouraged her. *She might be old but she's cool. She gets me, just like Aunty Mary does. I think I'll go to see her now. She seemed very down when I last spoke to her.*

All her aunts lived in reasonable proximity to her, so it was no trouble to walk round and visit them. As she approached the house, she noticed that the front room blinds were half-closed. Mary's car was parked in the driveway. Becca sauntered up towards the impressive entrance and stepped into a large, open porch. She rang the bell but there was no response. She buzzed it again but there was still no reaction. She thought she heard her cousin, Lisa, crying inside the house.

After five more attempts she was worried. Lisa's wailing became louder by the minute and Becca's anxiety increased. She looked through the window and screwed her eyes up to see through the slats of the partly open blinds. Lying on the floor was her aunty Mary, flanked by an empty bottle of pills and brandy. Quite a few loose tablets were strewn across the carpet. Lisa was kneeling at her mother's side, poking her shoulder to wake her up, oblivious to anything else.

"Mummy! Mummy! Mummy!" she cried.

Becca froze. Her heart was galloping in her chest wall. She knocked repeatedly on the window, but Lisa just ignored her. In her panic, Becca thought of breaking one of the panes to gain access into the house. Just as she was about to do so, the next-door neighbour came out of her door. Becca knew her reasonably well.

"Mrs. Rimmer, please help me!"

"What on earth's wrong, Becca?"

"It's Aunty Mary! She's… she's collapsed on the floor. I can't get in to help. Lisa's crying her eyes out and won't open the door."

"Oh, my word. I'm coming! Don't fret, dear. I've got a spare key."

Mrs. Rimmer gained entry and got a nasty shock when she saw Mary on the carpet.

"Now, Lisa and Becca, I'm going to phone for an emergency ambulance. Don't cry, it's the best thing to do."

She put a protective arm around Becca's shoulder and then rang for help. Lisa was sitting on the couch. She was inconsolable, her whole body quivering with fright.

"What about Uncle Don? He needs to know what's happening! I'm so scared."

"Now listen to me, Becca. The ambulance is on its way. What's your home telephone number? I'm going to call your mother as well to put her in the picture."

"Why is Aunty Mary on the floor with pills all over the place? Has she taken them? Has she? I can't bear it!"

"Shh, Becca, you're making Lisa even more upset. The sooner I tell your mother, the better."

Mrs. Rimmer left the girls and dialled the number in the hall, out of earshot.

Shirley was wondering where Becca was when the phone rang. *Where the heck is she? Probably playing Beatles records with all her friends somewhere. Beatles this and Beatles that. Will we all ever be Beatles-free?* She picked up the receiver and answered it in her up-market telephone voice.

"Hello, Mrs. Shirley Beacon here. Can I help you?"

"Hello, Mrs. Beacon. This is Mrs. Rimmer, your sister's next-door neighbour. I'm afraid I've got some rather upsetting news about Mary."

Shirley's heartbeat stalled and her tongue stuck to the roof of her mouth.

"Hello? Mrs. Beacon are you still there?"

"Yes. Oh, my word. What's happened to her?" asked Shirley with an overwhelming sense of dread.

"Well, it seems that your daughter, Becca, called round to see her and couldn't get into the house. She looked through the window and saw that Mary had collapsed on the floor and Lisa was hysterical, trying to wake her up."

"Collapsed! Is she still unconscious? Where are Lisa and Becca now?"

"In your sister's front room. I let myself in with a spare key that Mary gave me a while ago and I've phoned for an emergency ambulance."

"I'm coming over. Please, Mrs. Rimmer, look after Lisa and Becca until I get there."

"I will. But I need to tell you something. There's an empty bottle of pills on the floor. A few of them are scattered around the room. I hate to say this, but I think Mary has taken them with some alcohol and that's why she's spark out."

"Oh, dear God. I'm on my way."

Shirley pulled on her coat and pelted down the road. *Eric's got a job interview. I don't know how long he'll be. Please God, let Mary live. Oh, I'm so deeply upset. Poor Lisa. It's all about that good-for-nothing father of hers. The wrong one is lying on that floor. It should be him! Not my beloved sister. Hang on Mary. I'm coming, darling.*

Shirley arrived in record time to see the paramedics going into the house with a stretcher and medical equipment. By now, most of the neighbours had come out to see what was happening. They congregated in the street, huddled together with speculation.

Inside the house, the atmosphere was tense and fraught. Lisa and Becca hugged each other as the emergency response team fought to bring Mary round. Shirley walked in on the traumatic scene, and both Becca and Lisa ran into her arms.

"Is my mummy going to die?" sobbed Lisa.

"Shh darling, she's getting all the help she needs," replied Shirley, choking back the tears.

"But she looks so pale, and her lips are blue!"

"It's all right, Lisa. Just give them a chance. They're very good at their job."

The ambulance crew administered oxygen to support Mary's breathing, which was shallow. She had a slow heartbeat, and her blood pressure was low. They injected Naloxone into her bloodstream via her upper arm, in the hope of blocking the effects of her overdose. They put Mary into the recovery position on her side and kept her warm.

"Come into the dining room with me," urged Mrs.

Rimmer, who wanted to distract the girls away from the nervous tension.

"Thank you, Mrs. Rimmer. I'll stay here with Mary."

"Call me Alice, please."

"Thank you, Alice, for everything. I'm Shirley."

"Well, Shirley, I really pray that Mary will come through this. I always thought she was such a happy soul, but does anyone ever know what goes on behind closed doors? Can you contact her husband at all? I believe he's away, but this is a very serious situation and he should be told."

Shirley contemplated bitterly before she spoke. *Yes, he's away with his latest fancy-piece, cavorting in some hotel bedroom! He needs castrating!*

"Let's just deal with one thing at a time. My priority is Mary."

"Of course."

Shirley watched as the paramedics fought tirelessly to save her sister's life. Then miracle of miracles, Mary showed signs of improvement and was eventually stretchered out of the house and into the ambulance.

"She'll have to have her stomach pumped, but I think we got to her in time."

"Are you taking her to Crumpsall Hospital?" asked Shirley.

"Yes."

"May I come with? I'm her sister. Her husband's away… on business."

"That's fine. The doctors will be asking questions, so it's a good idea."

"Alice, would you be so kind as to take Lisa and Becca back to your house? I'll keep phoning home to see if my husband, Eric, has returned from an errand. He'll come and collect them as soon as possible. I'm sorry to drag you into this mess but I'm at my wits end. I want to thank you for all your help. Without you, this would have been a tragedy."

"Absolutely no problem whatsoever. Come with me, girls, I'll make you strong, sweet cups of tea. Now don't worry, because everything's under control," she said with a reassuring smile.

"Aunty Shirley, I want to go with mummy!" insisted Lisa.

"No, darling. She needs an adult with her to explain things. When your Uncle Eric picks you both up, you can come back and stay with us until your mum's better. So just pack a few things the while and we'll take it day by day. OK?"

"I want my dad. Do you know where he is?" asked Lisa, still trembling, but feeling somewhat calmer now that her mother was out of immediate danger.

"He's on the road but we'll find him." *The unfaithful, immoral brute!*

"He was nasty to mummy yesterday. They had a horrid row. It was over someone called Tracy. I think she's his secretary. Maybe she knows where he is right now."

Mary felt the bile rise in her throat. "Well, we'll look into all of it but now I have to go. Becca, please make sure that Lisa is OK."

"I will. When we get back home, she can listen to some Beatle records."

"Beatle records! Lisa needs peace and quiet, not burst eardrums! For once, Becca, can we please leave The Beatles out of our lives? Especially after such an upsetting situation!"

"That's just the point. Their music is magical and heals all bad thoughts."

"I don't care how ridiculously popular they are, now is not the time! Your aunty Mary is very unwell. Beatle records! I could scream, Becca! Enough!"

I do scream, Mum. All the time. For them. They are the answer. You just don't realise it. But I do. Their music will live forever and ever. Amen.

Chapter Three

Beatlemania invaded America on the 7th February 1964. They were waved off in their plane by thousands of screaming fans at London Heathrow airport and greeted with the same hysteria when they arrived at John F. Kennedy airport in New York. They initially appeared on *The Ed Sullivan Show*, and two nights later they played their first concert at the Washington Coliseum.

Becca broke down when they flew away in that mechanical monster. She thought she had lost them. As much as she was proud that they were on an international pedestal, she felt the familiar resentment of having to share her fixation with other fanatics. It was funny how each Beatle fan thought themselves the special one. That was the beauty of their existence. Every person became a someone. Every teenager had something identifiable. A sound of their own. A way of life. An escape. A story to tell their children.

It was the group's fifth single 'I Wanna Hold Your Hand' that had started the whole ball rolling out there. America played 'catch-up' and all their previous four hit singles dominated the charts at the same time. So, by the time they flew out, even though the US fans had never seen them in the flesh, they had five singles in their top ten. Suddenly, the States were ablaze with her property, on television coast to coast. The whole country succumbed to their domination. It was a British Beatle invasion and America had never seen anything like it before. But it would not stop there. Just like Becca had predicted to her aunty Doris, it spread like a musical pandemic.

Becca spoke to her bedroom walls. "I knew this would happen, John. Can you hear me, Paul? Do you realise you've opened the door for other British acts? And now you're selling yeah back to the yanks. Ha! But please come home soon. Don't stay away too long. I need you."

As she prophesied, in the future they would go on to gobble up Sweden, captivate Australia, devour New Zealand, conquer Germany, bewitch Italy, stun Japan, infiltrate the Philippines and beyond. This was a particular time in musical history when they would go from strength to strength, until the whole world surrendered on its knees.

Back in the present, the world premiere of their first feature film *A Hard Day's Night* took place at the London Pavilion on the 6th July 1964. All four Beatles, along with numerous important guests including Princess Margaret and Lord Snowden, attended.

Becca was besides herself when they flew from London to Liverpool, four days later, for the first northern

England screening. They were greeted upon their arrival at Speke Airport by three thousand screaming fans. Also on the 10th July, their third studio LP 'A Hard Day's Night' was released, with one side featuring songs from the soundtrack of the film of the same name. She had wanted to go to Liverpool and witness their triumph, but her mother put her size three, defiant foot down.

"I can be with Mikey! He's going to the airport with The Beacons! All his other friends will be there, too. Why can't I?" she'd protested.

"You're only thirteen! It'll be too crowded and dangerous, and that's that!"

"I'm fourteen in September!"

"It's barely July! Apart from that, even fourteen is still too young to be mingling with thousands of hysterical idiots. You could get crushed."

"There'll be loads of fans there, even younger than me!"

"I don't care! You're not going! Even your father agrees with me this time."

"I could go with Dad! Then we'll visit Uncle David and Aunty Rose afterwards. I know Liverpool so well. I've been travelling there and back since I was a little girl, in case you've forgotten."

"Knowing your way around Liverpool isn't the same as being in a crowded place with mass hysteria."

"You won't let me go to any of their concerts! They were in Manchester last year at the ABC Cinema. Twenty-five minutes away by car! You stopped me going then! It's not fair! I'm their biggest fan and I'm not allowed to go anywhere near them! Some of the girls in my class went with their older sisters or brothers. But not Becca Beacon!"

"Now listen to me. I've got other things to worry about that are far more important than this madness. Your aunty Mary is not good, and her marriage is on the rocks. She's recovering better than we thought, but she's still fragile. That good-for-nothing husband of hers has disappeared and your cousin Lisa is a mess."

"I get it. But Lisa told me that The Beatles' records help her to cope. Doesn't that prove something to you? Even though she's going through a very bad time she still listens to them, and their music helps her heal. Just like me. When I'm down or sad, their songs lift me up. I go into another world."

"You don't live in the real one! You need to grow up."

"You just told me I was only thirteen! A baby in your eyes."

"You know what I mean."

Becca had raised her eyes to the ceiling. *She'll never understand.*

"You're not stopping me from going to the pictures when *A Hard Day's Night* comes round, are you? Lisa wants to go as well."

"That's different. It's just a film. Your dad will drop you both off and then collect you when it's finished."

Becca ended up going to see her idols' feature film every day for a whole week, twice with her cousin Lisa, and then a variety of friends. Even her father accompanied her to two of the showings. The cinema was graced with her company nine times in all, because on two occasions she watched both the matinee and evening presentations. She knew every song on the soundtrack – all the lyrics, where to come in, each instrumental break, every expression and flick of their hair. She practically mimed the lines of each individual Beatle and their supporting cast. She memorised all the quips and punchlines, and relived the whole screenplay in her bedroom, with their pictures watching her. At school, she'd imitate them, speaking in a low Liverpudlian drawl, and her friends would split their sides laughing, as if she had actually written the script. She got two more detentions when caught in the act.

The history teacher, Miss Russell, was particularly annoyed. She had a Devonshire accent and Becca had perfected her voice, as she stood at the front of the class impersonating her, as an encore after her Beatles impersonation.

"Right now, you people, I said quickly and quietly, and the emphasis is on *quietly*! It's like a menagerie in 'ere. Now, you lot, stop going on about The Beatles! I've had a Beatle overdose. So, all of you, concentrate on Oliver Cromwell, and not John Lantern, Paul McIntosh, George Hairything and Ringo Starstruck."

The pupils howled with laughter but suddenly stopped when they saw Miss Russell in the doorway, watching Becca with a saturnine expression.

"Right now, Rebecca Beacon! This is a classroom, not a theatre. Detention!"

Not another one! Mum'll be hopping-mad. I'll have to tell her I've got after-school hockey practice. Miss Collins made me captain last week. At least she appreciates my sporty skills. Bloody teachers. Can't take a joke. I'm just having a laugh. Bummer!

*

In the summer holidays she travelled to Windsor for two weeks with her youth club. She'd been to the winter camp in Hertfordshire the previous year and made lots of friends from London. One girl, Tina, was particularly friendly and really excited to see Becca again.

"Hi Becca! I missed you. Thanks for replying to my letters," she enthused, with a great big hug.

"I missed you, too."

"Let's go and pick a bed in the dormitory. I want the one next to yours."

As they made their way into the building, a George Harrison lookalike smiled at Becca. She walked on then glanced behind, only to see that he was looking back at her. Lots of boys dressed like The Beatles to be in fashion, but this one resembled one of them.

He's so cool. I hope I see him again. Maybe I'll bump into him later.

In the evening all the youngsters were sitting and singing around the campfire. Becca joined in but did not think much of their taste. After nine verses of 'Ten Green Bottles' she'd had enough.

"How about a Beatles song?" she suggested when they stopped warbling.

"Yeah, yeah, yeah!" agreed Tina.

"Cue for a tune, if ever I heard one! Come on everybody! Let's do 'She Loves You'. Just give me a minute," enthused Becca, as she got up and ran through the door of the building.

"Where's she gone?" asked a few of them.

"I don't know," puzzled Tina.

In no time at all, Becca came running back with a tennis racket. She was breathless but stood in the middle of the large group.

"This is my guitar, so let's sing! Imagine that The Beatles are here on the grass! I'm their number one fan you know!"

Multiple voices shattered the stillness of the night, some tuneful and others tone deaf. But it did not matter a jot. Becca was in her Beatles element and threw herself into the spirit of the moment. She found it so thrilling belting out the words and dancing around the dying embers of the fire. She impersonated John and Paul, the way they sang and moved. Tina threw her head back and laughed. It was a spot-on imitation and Becca knew it, revelling in the limelight.

"How good was that?" she said breathlessly when it was over.

"Very good, Beatle girl," whispered a voice in her ear.

Becca turned round, to see the George Harrison lookalike.

"Oh!" was all she managed to muster.

He introduced himself. "I'm Terry Alexander, from the London crowd. That was some performance."

"I'm Becca Beacon, from Manchester."

"Beacon? Sounds like Beatle."

"I know. My brother Mikey's in a group called The Beacons. I thought of the name. They're so fab."

Terry smiled and Becca's heart flipped. *Gosh, he really looks like George. I wonder if he can sing?*

"Do you want to go for a walk?" asked Terry, interrupting her thoughts.

"Where?"

"Just around the grounds."

"Oh, OK," she agreed.

They left the scene and walked awhile, chatting away about different things but getting along well. Terry was the eldest of three siblings. He had a brother and sister who were too young to join the youth club but had every intention of doing so when they were older.

"How old are you?" he asked.

"I'm fourteen in September," replied Becca. Thirteen sounded far too babyish.

"I'm just fifteen. Mum and Dad threw a party for me last week. My birthday cake was so huge that the whole neighbourhood had a piece – and I live on a long road. Number sixty-three, to be exact."

Becca laughed. She looked very striking and animated. Her chestnut brown hair was shiny and framed her cheeky face. Her sparkling, large, brown eyes glittered in the semi-darkness and the skinny-rib jumper and tight jeans emphasised the swell of her blossoming figure.

After a long talk, they made their way back. It was getting late, and the youth leaders were instructing everyone to call it a day.

"Will I see you tomorrow?" asked Terry with a half-smile.

"If you want to. We're all going on a trip around Windsor Castle, are you?"

"I am now."

"Well, I'll see you in the morning," affirmed Becca, still holding her tennis racket.

"Definitely."

"You look like George Harrison."

"I've been told that a few times. Not a bad comparison, is it?" He grinned.

"A very good one."

"You're Beatles mad, aren't you?"

"Whatever gave you that idea?"

"I guessed."

"You're funny. Goodnight, George," she joked.

"Goodnight, Beatle girl."

Becca left him and her heart was singing. She really liked him and had a taste of her first real life crush. *He's lovely. So good-looking and easy to talk to. Even my mum would approve regardless of his Beatle looks. Roll on tomorrow.*

Tina was getting ready for bed in the dormitory when Becca came into the room.

"Where did you go? I've been looking everywhere."

"I went for a walk."

"On your own?"

"No, with George Harrison."

"You and your imagination," she laughed. "Anyway, I thought that John and Paul were your favourites. Have you changed your mind?"

"No way! But Terry is rather fab."

"Terry?"

"Terry Alexander."

"Who?"

"He's with your London group, we've been chatting and went for a walk together. He's coming on the trip tomorrow."

"Really?"

"You don't mind, do you Tina?"

"No. I'm just trying to picture him."

"He's the best looking one in the whole group. You can't miss him."

"Sounds cool."

Becca met up with Terry every day of the summer camp. He was very respectful of her age and treated her like a sister, but there was a spark between them. He kissed her on the cheek before she boarded the coach to go home and then saw her off, waving until she was out of sight. She felt sad but he promised to write and keep her up to date with all his news.

*

The minute she got back she needed a massive Beatles fix. While she unpacked, she listened to their 'Hard Day's Night' LP, singing along with her demigods at the top of her voice, intermittently kissing John and Paul on their pictured lips in between tracks. *Hey, you two pin-ups on my wall. Did you miss me? Hi George, I met your teenage double! He's called Terry and he sends his best wishes. Ringo, I missed you too. I love your drumming on the latest songs. You're all toppermost of the poppermost as John would say.*

While she had been away, her cousin Lisa's mental state had worsened. Becca's aunty Mary was finding it very hard to cope, and Lisa's condition only exacerbated her own depressive illness. When Becca was told, it brought her firmly back to earth with an almighty bump. As if that was not enough to contend with, 'uncle' pervert Ted and 'aunty' Jean had invited them all to their son's birthday party. Larry was really looking forward to seeing Becca in particular.

"Do I have to go?"

"Yes! Larry's missed you and he'll be very disappointed," admonished her mother.

"Has Mikey been invited?"

"Yes, but he can't go."

"Why is it OK for him not to go? Why can't I turn them down?"

"Because you and Larry are the same age and have been friends since you were babies."

"I know, Mum, but I told you before that I don't like his dad!"

"Why? What's your uncle Ted done that's so off-putting?"

"I wish you'd stop calling him my uncle! He's nothing to me!"

"Oh, Becca. We're all worried about your aunty Mary and Lisa, so a party is a welcome change. Don't spoil it for everyone. Also, your dad's found another job. He's over the moon about it, so he's got reason to celebrate. If you don't come, it'll put a damper on his good news. Look, you can even bring your Beatle records. I'm sure Aunty Jean will let you play them," she compromised.

Becca felt the familiar nausea at the thought of 'uncle' Ted and his wandering, sleazy hands. *I'll go but I'll keep well away from the creep. Anyway, Mum and Dad will be there so I can stay close to them. Mum's right about Larry. He'll be dead upset if I don't turn up. Oh, Larry, why have you got such a dirty old man for a dad? He needs locking up. I'll just ignore him. I realise now that he tries to control me. I can't tell Mum because she's got enough problems, and I wouldn't be able to tell Dad. I'd just die of shame. One day soon I'll just tell 'uncle' Ted to bugger off. Or kick him where it hurts!*

"OK, I'll come, and I'll definitely bring The Beatles LPs."

"Good. You know I love you very much, don't you?" said Shirley, as she kissed Becca's cheek. "If I go on about The Beatles it's because I don't want you in a dreamworld all the time."

"That 'dreamworld' is my safe place. John and Paul are my inspiration."

Becca never told her mother that she wrote her own lyrics about school life to the tunes of the current chart busters. Her parodies were always delivered with great feeling to the open-mouthed onlookers. The teachers would retire into their own private expressions of delight or disdain. Although she composed them for fun, it was in fact the beginning of her passion for future song writing. These creative moments were restricted for recreational bliss, but if they interfered with the dishing out of lectures, they were clamped down on like a ton of bricks.

As for her idols, following their two week appearance in the United States in early 1964, they became the most well-known group in America. In the six months that followed, they achieved seventeen Top 40 singles, including six number ones. Fans in the US now anticipated a country-wide tour.

While Becca had been at summer camp, they were in the middle of a world tour which started on the 4th June and ended on the 16th August. The day before they flew out, Ringo had felt ill at a photo session and fainted. He was hospitalised with a fever and diagnosed with acute tonsilitis. They'd all wanted to postpone the tour, especially George, but after much discussion they'd used a session drummer, Jimmy Nichol, to replace Ringo until he was well. They'd performed to hysterical, screaming, uncontrollable audiences in Denmark, The Netherlands, Hong Kong, and Australia. Ringo rejoined the group in Melbourne when he was well enough.

On the 11th and 14th of August they began recording sessions for what would become their fourth studio LP, 'Beatles for Sale'. They flew out to tour the US and Canada between 19th August and 20th September 1964, again to mass hysteria and pandemonium as Becca had so rightly predicted to her aunty Doris.

"I told you!" she said emphatically on another visit to her two aunts. "What did I tell you? Am I right or what?"

"The world's gone mad!" snapped her aunty Doreen.

"You ain't seen nothing yet! There's so much more to come," gushed Becca.

"How much more hysteria can we all take? The youth of today are crazy."

"You don't understand how amazing their music is, and what it means to people. It's so different and exciting. It makes me feel happy and free. On top of that, they look incredible. I really fancy John and Paul and have done from day one. What more can anyone wish for?"

"A Beatle-free planet," ridiculed Doreen.

"No, no, no! That would be a disaster. Even though I'm into other groups and singers, The Beatles are the ones that made it all happen in the way that it has. They've opened the door for British artists to be seen and heard in America. It was so hard before they did that. They're magical. I told Aunty Doris that ages ago, didn't I?"

"Yes, Becca. Yes, you did. I doubted you at the time but now I can see you were right," agreed Doris, looking at her with real love.

"Oh, don't encourage the girl, Doris! She needs to buckle down to her school lessons and show the teachers why she achieved her scholarship. Instead, what does she do? Rebels against anything and everything. An out-of-control radical with a head full of Beatles, Beatles, Beatles. I've no patience for any of this. Our Shirley is beside herself with worry about her," scorned Doreen.

"Er… excuse me, *she's* still here. I presume you're talking about me?" piped up Becca sarcastically.

"Less of the cheek, young lady."

"Less of the lecture, Aunty Doreen."

"See? See, Doris? She's our niece, but a cheeky young madam! What happened to the child we'd regularly take out for coffee and cake at the Kardomah Café? That little girl was a pleasure to be with. Warm, friendly, somewhat mischievous, but knew her place. Where's she gone?"

"She woke up," taunted Becca.

Doreen looked at Becca with an expression of disbelief and then spoke.

"Woke up? Woke up! To what exactly?"

"To music, art, and drama. To being free. To all things bright and beautiful. To feeling the wind in my hair. To soaring above the clouds. To red skies at night. To the lavender breeze. To poetry and songs. To being original. To being creative. But mostly, to John, Paul, George and Ringo."

"In your little dreamworld, are you aware of your aunty Mary and your cousin Lisa? They're going through hell," scorned Doreen.

"Of course! I see Lisa a lot. She probably talks to me more than anyone else! I help her cope, along with those Beatles that you hate so much! We listen to their records, and they lift her spirits. That's the effect they have on me, too. All bad thoughts are blown away. How good is that? It's better than seeing Lisa depressed."

"Poppycock! What about Aunty Mary? Do the four good-for-nothings lift her spirits as well?"

"That's so mean! In case you've lost your memory, I'm the one who saw her lying on the carpet with blue lips and her eyes rolled to the back of her head. Do you think for one minute I've forgotten? I have nightmares about her. I love her very much and pray that she gets well. It makes me cry to see how sad she is all the time. I go round and dread what I might find. The curtains are always drawn, and the house is a mess. There's about an inch of dust everywhere. I tidy up for them as much as I can. I even make her a meal because she hardly eats. Don't you ever say that I don't care! Don't you ever!"

A silence ensued after Becca's outburst. Doreen just mumbled something inaudible and went into the kitchen, her comfort zone. Becca's bottom lip trembled, and the tears began to flow.

"Oh, Becca. Don't cry. She didn't mean to upset you," sympathised Doris.

"Yes she did. She hates me."

"No. She just gets angry too quickly. Underneath all her harsh words, she does want the best for you."

"I doubt it."

"Your mother talks to us a lot. She's disappointed with your exam results because we all know that you're a clever girl and could do so much better. That's all. Nobody hates you, they just want you to succeed."

"Well, they've got a funny way of showing it."

"Listen to me, Becca. I understand you more than you think. I know you're a talented girl and that sooner or later those gifts will blossom. If I were you, I'd only go on about The Beatles to other fans. Not everyone sees them the way you do. Now, to your mum – who loves the big band era – they are the enemy. Just like Elvis was to Sinatra. I don't love their music the same as you do, but I can appreciate the way they make you feel."

"Oh, Aunty Doris. Why can't my mum be more like you?"

"I just told you why. Just keep your love for The Beatles close to your heart. Where better?"

"I'll try, but that will be very hard. They're in my blood so it's impossible to stop talking about them to other people. Especially those who need converting."

"Everyone is entitled to an opinion, Becca. You can't force your point of view on those who don't appreciate them."

"But they're missing out, big time."

"It's their choice. You must learn to respect that and move on."

"I don't get it! They should give them a chance. I'm sure my mum would love some of the songs on their LPs. They write beautiful ballads as well, you know. To be honest with you, I play the loudest rock songs on purpose to annoy her! There's a dent in the ceiling underneath my bedroom floor where she bangs the brush handle, while she's shouting to turn it down or switch it off!"

"Well then, if all she hears are rock songs blasting out, how would she know about the ballads? Why don't you ask her into your room and play them to her?"

"Mum and The Beatles are like chalk and smelly cheese. She can't stand their pictures on my wall for a start."

"Then play her the songs downstairs."

"Are you kidding? She's only got to look at their LP sleeve and she cringes. If she saw me carrying my record player down the stairs, she'd find an excuse to go out or clean the windows. Aunty Doris, she absolutely loathes them."

"What about your dad?"

"Dad's quite into them. He buys me all their records and books. That really gets on Mum's wick. What really bugs me is that Mikey plays his vinyl at full volume, but she never tells *him* off. Last week, The Beacons rehearsed in our garage. I mean, electric guitars plugged into amps. The bass was thumping away, and I felt the vibration in the house. Not to mention the drumbeats. Mum just made them cups of tea!"

"Now don't get upset. Mikey's more thoughtful. By that, I mean he doesn't go out of his way to annoy your mother. Also, he won't let his hobby interfere with his education."

"Well bully for him!"

"Becca, I'm trying to help you."

"By comparing me to my perfect brother?"

"None of us are perfect. We learn as we go along."

"Hmm."

"Now, would you like a nice cup of tea with some of your aunty Doreen's ginger cake?"

"I suppose. I can't resist that, even though she's a wet blanket."

"Becca!"

"I know, I know. Learn as I go along."

Doris smiled at her niece. *I love her dearly. She's very much her own person but I hope she grows out of this particular rebellious phase. I think she will in time. She's such an unusual girl. Maybe that's why I stick up for her so much.*

Becca was sitting on the couch when her aunty Doreen came in with tea and cake.

"I baked this yesterday, so it's moist and fresh. There's also some apple pie, so come and sit at the table Becca, please," she said cordially, putting all prior discord to one side.

"Aunty Doreen, I'm sorry. I didn't mean to be rude but what you said about Aunty Mary and Lisa was so hurtful."

"It was wrong of me. I shouldn't have been so critical. We don't see eye-to-eye, Becca, but I do care about you, in my own way. We all do."

"That's nice to know," she replied graciously.

Becca felt an unexpected warm glow as she reached for a second piece of her aunt's delicious ginger cake. *I can't expect them to understand my love of all things Beatles. For a start they're both ancient. But they're still family and I guess that's what matters. Anyway, I love Aunty Doris. As for school, well, that's all right for some. In my case it's such a drag. Mind you, the English lessons are good, and I love art and music. It's just the crazy rules. Sit up and be bored. Don't run down the corridor and make a noise. Don't forget to wear your hat and look like everybody else. Don't talk to your friends in lessons or get a detention. Don't be full of fun. Wipe your nose. Wear your indoor shoes indoors, and not on the grass! Straighten your tie! Comb your hair! Don't breathe!*

"Becca, do you want any cream with your apple pie?" asked Doreen, interrupting her thoughts.

"Mm, please. Your baking is wonderful. Nobody can bake like you. Not even my mum."

Doreen gave a half-smile, which for her was the equivalent of a wide grin. Becca saw a long-forgotten twinkle in her eye that had got lost along the way. Life had a habit of stealing dreams.

Nobody is going to rob me of my dreams, and I'll always love The Beatles. Whatever happens.

Chapter Four

The Beatles' fourth studio LP, 'Beatles for Sale', was released on the 4th December 1964. The sessions also gave birth to a single, 'I Feel Fine', backed by 'She's a Woman'. They had been non-stop all year, touring and recording, both home and away. By this time, the whole world knew their names. Becca was ecstatic, even with the screeching sound of the accidental feedback at the beginning of their latest single.

As per usual, her dad had bought her the latest records and she flew up the stairs to hear their unbeatable offerings. She'd sit there with a pen and paper, jotting down the lyrics, playing the songs over and over, until she was familiar with all the words.

Beatlemania was at its peak in 1964, with radio and television engagements and endless promotion. Their manager, Brian Epstein, explained that no group today would come off a long US tour at the end of September, go into the studio and start a new LP, still writing songs, and then go on a UK tour, finish the LP in five weeks, still touring, and have the LP out in time for Christmas.

Becca thought they were working too hard. As much as she bathed in their fanatical spotlight by proxy, she felt they would be exhausted by the end of the year.

"It's too much," she said to the photographic wall. "John and Paul, slow down a bit. I know you're both incredible but enough is enough. It'll wear you out. George and Ringo, too."

Around this time, she was spending her time sketching portraits of different pop personalities, especially The Beatles. She sold them to other pupils for half a crown – two shillings and sixpence in old currency. The art teacher, Miss Cropper, thought she could put her talents to better use and told her so.

"You're gifted, Rebecca. Try diversifying and paint landscapes, as well as faces. You seem to stick to the same old theme. A little birdie told me that you get paid for your efforts. That's wrong! Half of your sketches are missing, so I know it's true. I should really report you to the headmistress. I'll just give you a ticking off this time, but make no mistake, I'll have to blow the whistle if you do it again. Oh, fasten your tie, comb your hair and make sure you polish your shoes tomorrow."

"Yes, Miss." *Anything you say, Miss. I thought art teachers were trendy. Are you sure you're not in the armed forces in your spare time? I'll give you something different all right.*

Out of mischief, Becca began drawing hands and feet. Pages and pages of them, especially feet. Everything else went out of the well-balanced window. When Miss Cropper came round to her desk to inspect her work, she was momentarily speechless.

"I promise not to sell these to anyone, Miss. Not even to those with a foot fetish," she mocked, fluttering her eyelashes.

"Rebecca Beacon, you're a very cheeky girl. Detention!"

"That brings the total to a round figure of four so far this term. Carry on like this and I'll win a prize. Possibly a year's supply of shuttlecocks, or even ping pong balls. I'm pretty good at all things sporty. I've always thought that we should add badminton and table tennis to the curriculum. It's good to plan ahead."

"Another detention!"

"Oh, thank you very kindly. That makes five."

"Rebecca Beacon, go and stand in the corner, right now!"

"With a dunces cap?"

"Go!"

"Yes, Miss Cropper. How long should I stay there?"

"Until I decide. And stop answering me back!"

"Not a word. Not a word."

Some of the other pupils looked at Becca and began to giggle, not at her, but with her.

"And we'll have less of *that* or else you'll *all* get a detention," derided their teacher.

Becca stifled a fit of laughter as she gazed at the classroom wall. *She's so uptight! I know I'm good at sketching portraits, so what's the big deal if I sell them? Is the world going to come to an end? She needs to buy John Lennon's book,* In His Own Write. *I've read it about one hundred times since it was published at the beginning of the year. His poems, short stories and illustrations make me laugh. She probably wouldn't rate it anyway. You have to be bonkers to appreciate it. So, count me in!*

Miss Cropper ignored her for the rest of the lesson. When the bell rang for lunch, Becca was still standing there, in an empty classroom. Just as she was about to go into the refectory, her teacher appeared out of nowhere, holding a ruler.

"Come here, Rebecca, and hold out your hand, palm-side up."

"So, you want to hold my hand? Fab!" she trilled.

"I'm going to punish you for your insolence! And stop making references to Beatles songs. It's tedious and pointless. You really are a thorn in my side."

"But I thought you rated my work."

"I do. But you've brought *this* on yourself."

Becca winced as she felt the sharp sting of the ruler on the underside of her hand. Her palm was red from the painful contact, but she did not complain.

"I could have given you five strikes to match the number of detentions you were bragging about beforehand! Now, go and have your lunch because it's getting late. No hunched shoulders, straighten your tie and don't run down the corridor."

"Yes, Miss Cropper." *Bitch.*

"That's a good girl. You've got a gift for painting and sketching, so please use it to further your career."

"Yes, Miss Cropper." *Up yours.*

"Good."

Becca joined her friends in the school canteen. They

were totally on her side about the ruthless ruler.

"I thought she was an artist. Turns out she's a sadist," complained Becca, feeling the after-effect of her punishment.

"It shouldn't be allowed," said a blonde, bespeckled friend called Jane. "We should be able to report them for abuse."

"I think I'll write a parody called 'Straps, Rulers and Detentions.'"

"I got a detention the other day for just laughing in class," complained Jane. "I only asked Sally if I could fill my fountain pen with her ink, as mine had run out. I made a mess of it and giggled."

"Pathetic."

"Isn't it just?"

"What's on the menu?" asked Becca, smelling the air for a clue.

"Fish and chips, followed by apple pie and custard."

"Sounds good. What it tastes like is another matter."

"Hey Becca, have you listened to the Fab Four's latest LP. You know, 'Beatles for Sale'?"

"About one thousand times."

"What do you think?"

"I think they just get better and better. I'm in awe of their talent. The songs are amazing. Not to mention their looks."

"Who's your favourite Beatle?"

"I can't decide between John and Paul, so I'll say both of them."

"I think Paul's the most handsome," sighed another friend called Lynne.

"Yeah, but John's so sexy and dynamic. You'd know if he was in the room," enthused Becca.

"If only!" swooned Jane, and they all laughed.

"Have you ever seen them in concert?"

"No. My mum's always stopped me. But I'll tell you something, next time they come to Manchester, I'll be on the front row. I don't care if I'm grounded for a year. I'm going!"

"Good for you! We can all go together!" Lynne suggested.

*

Mathematics was the first lesson after lunch. Algebra, number theory, geometry, and arithmetic did not float her boat, although she was quite adept at adding and subtracting in her head as well as on paper.

The maths teacher, Mr. Jones, was her worst enemy. He knew her failings and seemed to show great delight in the fact. Just to add more fuel to the rebellious situation, she had brought with her some glass beads that her mother had worn on stage when she used to sing. Becca remembered how they shone under the spotlight as her mum charmed the audience. She wore them round her neck, and they dangled down over her school tie as she sat demurely on the permanently uncomfortable chair. *I've got cramp in my bum from the hard wood.*

Mr. Jones did not notice them at first, but when he did, he went in for the arithmetical kill.

"Rebecca Beacon! What on earth are you wearing?"

"Sir?"

"You heard me!"

"My uniform."

"Round your neck! What are you wearing round your neck?"

"Oh, you mean my mum's beads."

"Take them off. Now!" he snorted with flared nostrils.

"But they're so pretty, sir."

"Get up! Come to the front of the class!"

"Yes, sir."

As she made her way, she heard the usual stifled giggles from her fellow pupils. She winked at her friend, Jane, who was on the verge of silent hysterics.

"Now, are you going to take them off? Or else I'll do it for you!"

"That's kind of you, sir. Whatever you think best."

He snorted even louder as he yanked them off, breaking them in the process. Multiple glass beads rolled across the floor, under the desks, and over the length and breadth of the room.

"Now look what you've done!"

"But *you* did it, sir."

"I want you to pick up every one of those beads, so on your knees, *right now*! You really are a pain in the neck!"

"My mum will be upset. They're sentimental, you see. But I think they can be rethreaded. She's very skilled at making things by hand. Then I can wear them again. Around the pain in my neck."

"On your knees, Rebecca Beacon, and after you've picked them up, I want you to go to see the headmistress for a suitable punishment!"

"I know the way."

"*Pick them all up!*"

Becca managed to collect the beads and placed them into a tidy pile. Mr. Jones sat red-faced and silent throughout the whole process.

"Have you got anything I can put them in, sir?" she asked politely.

"Where's your briefcase?"

"Under my uncomfortable chair."

"Then plonk them in there!"

"Plonking good idea."

"Rebecca Beacon, you are impudent and out of control."

"Apparently."

"That's it! Class, be quiet and practice your geometry until I get back."

He frog-marched Becca to Mrs. Shaw's study. She prepared herself for the umpteenth lecture from she-who-must-be-obeyed, who sat on her throne looking like Mary I of England, reigning in her own right rather than through marriage to a king.

"Rebecca. I hear you've been a very naughty girl again. I have no alternative but to give you the strap. It pains me to keep on doing this and seeing no remorse for your actions."

"It pains me even more, Mrs. Shaw." *That rhymes.*

"Why are you always looking for trouble? You're a very bright pupil who could do much better if you concentrated on your lessons instead of entertaining the class. You got high marks in your last English language exam, and you excel at English literature. Why can't you apply that motivation to all your other subjects?"

"Because I'm not interested in all of the other subjects."

"This school prides itself on all-round ability. I notice that you got 97% in your last chemistry exam but a very low mark in maths. How's that possible?"

"I memorised it."

"Are you sure that you didn't cheat?"

"No. I told you. I memorised it all."

"Impossible."

"I've got a photographic memory. Once I set my mind on something, I don't even have to understand it. I just remember everything."

"Hmm."

"I know the script to *A Hard Day's Night* from beginning to end."

"*A Hard Day's Night*?"

"Yes. The Beatles feature film."

"Aha! Those Beatles! I believe you're utterly obsessed with them."

"They're everything to me."

"Listen to their records out of school but don't bring their disruptive influence into your lessons. Personally, I can't see the attraction. It's mass hysteria on a global scale."

"The Beatles aren't disruptive. They're bloody marvellous."

"Rebecca, don't swear!"

"Sorry, Mrs. Shaw." *Flake off.*

She dipped into the drawer of torture and brought out the dreaded strap.

"Now, put your hand out."

"Why? It's not on fire, is it?"

"Rebecca! Do as I say! Those cheeky retorts are the reason you're being punished."

She raised the broad-leather strap, with the hard handle, and gave Becca two huge swipes on her left palm, which made her flinch.

"Now. Go back to your maths lesson and do try to avoid getting more detentions. Your house is most unhappy with the black marks against their name."

"Yes, Mrs. Shaw."

"Oh, Rebecca. Mr. Jones has also given you a detention. I suggest you make a note in your diary for next Wednesday. This week's chock-a-block with all the others!"

"Will do."

"Please try and behave. You're not an unmanageable pupil in a violent sense, but your attitude leaves a lot to be desired. For some reason you abuse your capabilities. We wish to give all our pupils the best education possible, so that they can go forward into a productive future."

"Hmm."

"Do you understand?"

"I do and I don't."

"What do you mean?"

"I think that if a pupil excels in one or two subjects, then the teacher should praise them. This all-round ability rule is wrong. We can't be good at everything."

"But you can, Rebecca, if you apply yourself. What do you want to do when you leave school? If you wish to go to university, you will have to get high grades in your A-Levels when the time comes. Before that you must take your O-Levels, and it would be so beneficial if you knuckled down now so that you are well-prepared for both sets of examinations."

"I want to sing and write songs."

"You want to what?"

"Sing and write songs."

"Are we talking classical songs, or ear-splitting ones?"

"I don't know yet."

"Can you read music?"

"No."

"Then you need to learn."

"The Beatles don't read music, but it doesn't stop them."

"I wish something would! I've never seen anything like the ridiculous hysteria that surrounds them. Young people need role models, not four mop tops screeching out their so-called songs. They whip up mayhem and it leads to rebellion."

"You sound like my mother."

"Your mother is correct."

"That's debatable."

Mrs. Shaw sighed deeply. She studied Becca's face and saw absolute defiance in her eyes. *She's such an intelligent girl with a self-destruct button waiting to be pressed. She could go far but is abusing her education. She's not the only one obsessed with those Beatles. I've had to caution quite a few of the pupils about their fixation interfering with their lessons and homework. What is it about that blasted group? The sooner they fade away the better for all concerned.*

"All right, Becca. You can go now. But I don't want to see you in my study again. Please try and behave yourself and don't answer back! That's the key. Keep your opinions and sarcastic remarks to yourself. Just buckle down and learn. I have faith in your abilities. Don't disappoint me."

"Yes, Mrs. Shaw."

Becca left the room, deep in thought. Not about her educational syllabus but about her own desire to embrace all things theatrical.

They just don't get it. They never will. But I know what I want and I'm going in my own direction. It's a calling. The Beatles have shown me the way. I know them so well but it's hard to believe that they don't know me. They do in my imagination, so I'll settle for that. They belong to the world now. That's so exhausting. They must feel the pressure. Writing, recording and touring endlessly. Screaming fans, drowning out their songs. When they do their next UK tour, I'll be there! Oh, yes! Front row seat. In touching distance of them. Oh, my goodness. The thought of it makes me weak.

*

Becca's whole life pattern at that time was made up of going to school and coming home, with weekends as an escapist attraction. They were composed of Beatle books and 'Ringo Rolls' with cheese for breakfast. She strolled through the park with an ear-hugging transistor, flirted with the boys, and danced in beat clubs, always lying about her age to gain entry. She trained her long, straight fringe to lie decoratively on her curled eyelashes. She compared collections of Beatle pictures and listened to their records religiously every Sunday afternoon with a close group of friends. They all had their opinion on the songs. Becca dismissed them because she was the Beatle expert.

When she really thought about these episodes in her life, she was amazed at her total involvement with The Beatles scene, only she never considered herself as 'part' of the situation. She was always different from the other fanatics and there was not an event or fact about the group that escaped her. She was like a half-crazed Beatle junkie, buying and selling information.

She still travelled with her father to visit her Uncle David and Aunty Rose in Liverpool. Every pavement flag she trod on might have once felt the weight of a Beatle footstep. She could see their faces in shop doorways and windows. Even at the hectic bustle of New Brighton fairground, they rallied round her. They waved to her with each exciting rotation from the big wheel. They shouted to her from every perilous drop of the figure eight rollercoaster. They hid in between the spirals of the helter-skelter.

Even now she loved riding the ferry across the legendary Mersey, watching the industrial sunset of rusty crimson and orange merging with the metallic grey of the evening sky. She felt closer to her dream than ever before as she neared the iconic silhouette of the Liver Buildings and gazed upon that city of musical genius. She remembered how she felt as a child. Her earliest recollection of any great body of water was the Mersey-kind, covered in ferry foam. She wanted to clasp it all in her arms, but realised there was too much water. But there was always that dangerous invitation to challenge the hidden secrets of its depth.

Becca had written a short poem about the river and its boats. She mulled it over in her head:

Chugging, gliding, sailing, racing,
Swirling, skating, riding, pacing,
Chasing, blowing, seagulls choking,
Captains smiling, most beguiling,
Liners lining, ferries filing,
Tugboats dragging, cargo sagging,
Stormy weather, pull together,
Sunny harbour, dockside father,
Sirens wailing, never failing,
Anchors grating, sailors waiting.

*

She had recently received her 'Beatles Christmas Record' from the fan club and played it repeatedly at the weekend. They were all talking, joking, and laughing together with a message to their countless admirers. Her toes curled up when she heard John's deep voice. She loved everything about him and identified with his whole persona. At the same time, she adored Paul and every single thing about him. *When people ask me who's my fave Beatle, I say both of them. The other day, Jane asked, "If John walked to the left, and Paul to the right, which one would you follow?" I told her that I'd have to cut myself in half.*

While she was in the middle of her musical reverie the postman arrived with quite a few letters. Amongst them was one from her George Harrison lookalike boyfriend. They wrote regularly to each other, and Becca had learnt a lot about him through their correspondence.

"Becca. There's a letter for you from Terry," her mother called out to her from the bottom of the stairs. "Come on down and have some lunch."

Shirley was quite pleased about Terry. Even though Becca was fourteen, she thoroughly approved of the connection. She liked the fact that they had met at summer camp under supervision. Also, Becca had shown her some of his letters and it was obvious from his style of writing that he was intelligent and very polite.

Becca sat at the table and opened up the envelope. She read its contents with zeal and gave a little sharp intake of breath before she spoke.

"Mum, he's coming down this way next weekend to see me! He's visiting some relatives in Bury and wants us to meet up."

"That's lovely. Ask him here."

"Can I? That'd be great. I've missed him."

"Well, he's obviously missed you."

"You'll like him, Mum, even though he looks like George."

"Is that why *you* like him?"

"Well, it helps."

Shirley laughed regardless of her dislike of all things Beatles.

"Becca Beacon, you're one on your own."

"Oh, I do hope so."

"Have your beans on toast before they get cold."

Shirley shook her head with affectionate disbelief. Her daughter was an enigma, but she loved her dearly, regardless of their difference of opinion. She was becoming almost acclimatised to her musical fixation. After all, it had been two years since the whole thing started and if Shirley was honest with herself, she inwardly realised that the whole world had joined in with Becca's addiction.

When I watched them on The Morecambe & Wise Show, I actually thought they were quite good. Then when they joined Eric and Ernie to sing Moonlight Bay, I was rather impressed. I hid that from Becca. I still think John Lennon is sarcastic in his interviews. He's always got something controversial to say. Come to think of it, so's Becca. Maybe she's modelled herself on him. Mind you, she was never backward at coming forward. She can wrap her father round her little finger. She was a loving but mischievous little girl. Hmm. Perhaps Lennon is a kindred spirit rather than an influence.

Shirley was spot on with her contemplation. Becca did have the same opinions, feelings and interests as John. She was very drawn to him in that respect. She never copied him, she just bonded with him, albeit from a distance. She instinctively knew that the fame was now backfiring and causing him pressure. She could tell by his antics on stage that he was becoming frustrated with the adoring audience, specifically the screaming. The hysterical response of the fans could be heard above the songs. Also, the constant touring, television appearances, interviews and other relentless itineraries were hard to endure.

Becca had an intuition way beyond her years. She was very perceptive even as a child, bordering on psychic. She knew from the second she heard 'Love Me Do' that the group were destined for great things. The hairs on the back of her neck also stood to military attention when she first clapped eyes on them a few weeks later. It was more than a twelve year old girl's crush. It was as if the universe had whispered into her ear to expect a musical earthquake.

She had just finished writing another poem. It was anarchic but very relevant. As usual, she had memorised it in full, and recited it mentally in her fourteen-year-old head.

Said the teacher to the pupil
You're nothing but pie up in the sky
You couldn't care less about the way you dress
I'll clip your wings before you fly
Said the pupil to the teacher
Well, you're just talking through your head
You couldn't give a damn about the way I am
You know you'd rather see me dead – to the world.
Oh, no, girl, you've got me wrong
I only want to show you that life is long
Without an element of discipline
It's hard for you to see beyond the mess you're in
Forget the music and the fantasy
'Cos you're just going to lose your sanity
Just follow me into the lion's den
I guarantee you'll never wonder why again.
Said the pupil to the teacher
Don't waste your energy or time
I'd rather sing than be pulled by a string
I'd sooner taste the sweeter wine
Said the teacher to the pupil
You've got your head beneath the sand
You'd never come through if it was up to you
You really need a helping hand – in the world

Oh, no, sir, you've got me wrong
I only want to show you that death is long
Without an element of poetry
It's hard for you to see beyond the life you lead
Forget the lectures on society
'Cos you're going to lose your own identity
Just follow me into the sun and rain
I guarantee you'll never wonder why again.

She laughed to herself as she pictured reading it to Mr. Jones. His neck and face would go blood red with rage. It was far more rebellious than the broken glass beads. She was sorely tempted to slip it into his desk drawer. She giggled out loud at the thought. *Stick that in your parallelogram and smoke it! I should cocoa. I'm going places. So, watch this space, sir!*

She thought deeply about the youth culture of her generation. *I'm not a mod or a rocker. Ringo said he was a mocker! But that was originally one of John's quips. I'm a rebel but I'm not violent. Mum should take note and thank her lucky stars that I wasn't involved with that clash in Brighton earlier in the year.*

She mulled over the mods and rockers subculture battle that had taken place on the 18th May. The rockers were all about motorcycling and wore black leather jackets and 'brothel creeper' boots. They were heavily influenced by Marlon Brando in the 1953 film *The Wild One*. Their music genre revolved around 1950s rock and roll. Artists such as Gene Vincent and Eddie Cochran.

The mods were very into fashion, as well as music. They rode scooters and wore suits, or sharp outfits. Their favourite musical genres were Motown, soul, ska and British blues-rooted bands like The Who, The Small Faces and The Yardbirds.

Conflicts between the two occurred at Clacton and Hastings during last Easter weekend. A second battle had taken place on the south coast on the Whitsun weekend of the 18th to 19th May, especially in Brighton, where violent fighting occurred over the two days, then moved along the coast to Hastings and back. The newspapers described the mods and rockers clashes as being of 'disastrous proportions'. As a consequence of the media coverage, two MPs visited the areas to survey the damage and called for a resolution to control hooliganism.

Mum and Dad were horrified by the coverage. I kind of understood where it was all coming from in terms of rivalry, but I didn't agree with the fighting. My sun sign is Libra. I believe in peace harmony and justice. So no, I'm not a mod or a rocker. I don't need any labels. I don't follow the crowd. I'm my own person.

The Beatles have a massive fanbase worldwide. I know I'm only one of the members, but I was one of the first. I haven't jumped on a Beatles bandwagon. If anything, the bulk of the fans have jumped on mine! I'm not just a fan. I'm not just a follower. I'm a kindred spirit.

I know I'm going to have a career in music. Either that or I'll write books. Or both. So, in the meantime I'll just play the game of life. Day by day.

The school career convention will do nothing for me. I have a calling. It's not just a whim. It's a fact.

Chapter Five

1965 was knocking at the door. This was to be Becca's year of mini-skirts, a revolution in fashion, Ringo's marriage, Bob Dylan, Winston Churchill's funeral, The Beatles' MBEs, John and Paul's TV special and her much-awaited live Beatle concert, which she attended two months after her fifteenth birthday.

Before all that occurred she was still the classroom clown, happy enough to entertain her fellow pupils. But not long into the year, she was bitterly jolted from her recreational paradise. The career convention swooped down on her fairyland like a slavering vulture. It pecked at her brain until it bled with anguish.

Up until then it had been 'Beatles and Beacons' – those irreplaceable beacons of light always shining through the darkness. For the first time in her life, she began to think of the future in real terms. The realisation was so shattering that she thought somebody had smacked her across the face. Her parents attended the assembly with her because they wanted a way forward that would suit her needs.

Becca listened to the boring lecturer explaining the endless opportunities that would be available to her through her grammar school education. Her mind whirled with the prospect of a conventional future, and she never felt more deflated. She did not gravitate towards any of the choices. They left her stone cold.

She had tinkled around with her friend's piano and could play chords. It was instinctive rather than technical. The same with an acoustic guitar. For some weird reason she mastered them on the day that Winston Churchill died. The 24th January 1965, to be exact. Her parents were not impressed, and anyway, they were upset by Churchill's demise.

Then Ringo married Maureen Cox on the 11th February. Brian Epstein was his best man and George was a witness. Becca mentally wished them all the best when she watched it on the news.

On the 9th April, The Beatles released their new single 'Ticket to Ride'. The flip side 'Yes It Is' was another example of three-part harmony at their best. News of their second feature film, *Help!*, filtered through the Beatle airways. Before that, they toured Europe.

Help! Was released on the 29th July. The plot was about the group struggling to protect Ringo from both an eastern cult and a pair of wackadoodle scientists, all of whom were obsessed with retrieving a sacrificial ring sent to him by a fan. The film was shot on Salisbury Plain, London, the Austrian Alps, and both New Providence Island and

Paradise Island in the Bahamas. Their fifth studio album and the soundtrack to the film, of the same name, was released on the 6th August. After that they toured America from the 15th to 31st August.

Becca would lap it all up, but it would be marred for two reasons. Firstly, she thought that they were under relentless pressure, and secondly her own situation was complicated and causing her anxiety. *I really don't know which way to turn. Before the career convention I was so sure of everything, but now I realise that it's a bit of a pipe dream and not so easy. Bob Dylan's song 'The Times They Are A-Changin' is fantastic and says it all really. He's so brilliant. A true wordsmith.*

Becca read that The Beatles had met Bob Dylan on the 28th August 1964 after playing a show at Forest Hills Tennis Stadium in New York, but she did not realise that he had 'introduced' them to marijuana. The two parties were brought into contact by a mutual friend, the writer and journalist Al Aronowitz. In the 'swinging sixties' they were all smoking pot, but they had to be cautious not to get on the wrong side of the law.

Her brother Mikey had experimented with several joints, together with his circle of musical buddies. Becca knew there was something weird going on when she tried to talk to them. They were giggling over nothing, and their eyes were permanently glazed.

"Hey, Mikey! Here comes the little sister. Best be careful, man. Is she a grass?" laughed the insufferable Mick Jagger lookalike called Alan.

"She's cool. She's cool," repeated Mikey, whose vision was out of focus.

"Who do you dig, little sister? The Stones or The Beatles?"

"The Beatles," she shot back without hesitation, although she did rate The Rolling Stones highly.

"They're on the way out, man," Alan derided. "Finished, caput, big time."

"In your dreams, man," she mocked.

"They look like fucking puppets! I mean, who wears identical suits today on stage and bows down after each song? They're unhip! Overrated! Over here, there and everywhere. Bye-bye Beatles. Hello, Stones. Dig?"

"The Beatles will never die, even when they're dead! Their music will live on. Their influence will continue after all of us have gone," she prophesised.

"Whoa! Cool it, little sister."

"The name's Becca, and I'm a person in my own right. Dig?" she mocked again.

"Leave her alone, Alan. She's been a fan since she was twelve," verified Mikey.

"And how old is she now? Twelve and a half?" he flouted.

"And how old are *you,* apart from being too big for your boots?" she pilloried.

"Feisty little sister, aren't you?"

"Faulty little mister, aren't you?" she ridiculed.

"I said leave her alone," reiterated Mikey.

"I can defend myself, Mikey. Jumped-up Jagger lookalikes do nothing for me. He's a first-class limelight hogger," she spurned, fluttering her eyelashes in a sarcastic fashion.

"Give her some weed. She needs to get high," insisted Alan.

"No thanks. I'm high on imagination. That's my fix. Oh, and the 'on the way out' Beatles. They're better than any magic bullet. So, you see, I'm self-reliant. Are you? Man."

Alan's mouth dropped regardless of his drug-induced state, and Mikey burst out laughing. Becca sang one verse of 'I Don't Want to Spoil The Party', took a bow, stuck her tongue out, and left.

"You won't get the better of my Beatle-mad sister. She's as sharp as a tack. John Lennon's her mentor. Or maybe she's his. Either way, she's a rebel with a cause. You asked for it, Alan. Oh man, does she rock!" he chortled.

"I hope she doesn't grass," frowned Alan.

"Grass about the grass?"

"Don't you start!"

"Nah, she won't tell. You rubbed her up the wrong way," said Mikey, still grinning.

"She's on something," said another friend called Ralph.

"Yeah, her high horse," replied Alan, sardonically.

"Becca's Becca. She'll always come out smelling of rebellious roses."

"Anyway, have you got any more spliffs? She's left a bad vibe, man."

Mikey laughed even more. He was very fond of his sister and thought she was unique. He knew that she was forever in trouble at school. She had told him all about her disdain for rules and lectures. He was much more compliant because he wanted to study the history of art and was determined to the get high grades in his exams. Besides, he liked the bulk of his teachers and they warmed to him. However, he thought the strap was brutal. He had seen the red weal on the palm of her hand from the blows.

"It should be banned," he had said angrily when she told him all about the punishments.

"Never mind, Mikey. I'll find a way out, and one day, when I'm riding high, they'll all be sorry. There's no excuse for abuse." *I've had enough of that up the bloody road with 'uncle' touchy-feely Ted. He tried to corner me the other day and I told him to get lost. He just laughed. He makes me feel sick. I believe in karma. What goes around comes around.*

*

In June 1965, Queen Elizabeth II appointed each of The Beatles an MBE, following their nomination by Prime Minister Harold Wilson, who had persuaded the Queen to honour the group. It was a controversial decision because this was usually bestowed on military veterans and civic leaders of the time.

On the 26th October, all four of them went to Buckingham Palace to receive their medals. Rock music still had a negative undercurrent in society and the reaction from many previous recipients was foreseeable. Several returned their decorations as a mark of opposition. Colonel Frederick Wagg sent back the twelve medals he had earnt fighting in both World Wars and went on to resign from the Labour Party. He thought that decorating The Beatles would make a mockery of everything the country stands for, and their playing and singing was terrible.

As a result of all the criticism, it was rumoured they were so nervous at the idea of meeting the Queen that they went to the bathroom and smoked pot. Despite the formality, The Beatles still signed autographs for numerous other recipients, including one man who told Paul that he wanted his signature for his daughter, but he didn't know what she saw in him! Thousands of screaming fans were outside Buckingham Palace and went hysterical when they arrived. One girl actually scaled the railings, and the police had an unenviable job holding back the out of control crowds. Beatlemania had struck again. Becca watched the news and felt pride and envy simultaneously.

I wish I was there to see them close-up. Mind you, I wouldn't like to be squashed against those railings. I'd prefer it if I was in their car! Squashed up against them!

When The Beatles' feature film, *Help!*, was shown in the summer holidays, Becca went every single day to watch her boys in colour. She noticed that John had put on quite a bit of weight, but he was still her long-distance, sexy soulmate. Her sixth sense told her that he was unhappy. Even though he was smiling and joking throughout the whole of the film, she saw beneath the façade. The words of the song were a cry for help, and she wondered why. The more she viewed the picture, the more she felt his pain.

When she told her friends, they thought she was exaggerating and reading far too much into the situation.

"He looks great! Yeah, he's a bit heavier but he's still the joker in the pack," said Jane.

"What are you talking about, Becca? His voice is better than ever, and he's having fun," added Sally.

"He's not having fun. He's troubled."

"Oh, Becca. I know you love him and Paul, but you don't really *know* them. I mean none of us do. Just enjoy their music and the way they look. They're gorgeous and they thrill me. That's all that matters."

"They're human. Not machines."

Sally rolled her eyes and Jane did the same.

"He's married to Cynthia and they have a lovely little boy, Julian, to keep him warm and safe," insisted Jane.

Becca nodded, but in her mind she heard a warning bell. *Maybe my imagination is working overtime. But I do get feelings about things, and they happen.*

"Anyway, I'm excited about their programme for Granada TV," enthused Sally.

"What's that, then?" asked Jane.

"It's a television special called *The Music of Lennon and McCartney.* John and Paul will be in Manchester on the first and second of November recording it, and I, for one, will be wagging school to be there," interjected Becca.

"You can't! The teachers will explode! Not to mention your mum and dad!" gasped Jane.

"All the more reason to go! Do you think I'm going to pass up an opportunity to see them in the flesh? No way! I'll be there at the crack of dawn."

"Oh, Becca. We've all booked tickets to see them in concert in December! My heart's beating so fast at the thought. Isn't that enough? We'll be there! Under the same roof! Watching them sing! Oh, my goodness, it's too much to bear. I'm ticking off the days."

"Me too, but I still need an extra fix, before the big fix. So, it's off to Granada I go with high hopes of seeing them close-up."

"You'll be in school uniform."

"I'm packing my denim jacket and matching mini-skirt, skinny-rib top, kitten-heel shoes, and make-up in my sports bag. Mum won't suspect a thing. I'll stop off at Victoria station, get changed, then leave my bag in luggage storage. I'm not meeting my two heartthrobs looking like I've just got off the school bus. I want them to think that I've just stepped out of Biba."

*

True to her word, on the morning of Monday 1st November 1965, Becca left for school, or so everyone thought. She took the train to its terminus and made her way to the public toilets, where she undressed and got changed into her trendy outfit. She put on foundation, mascara, eyeshadow and lipstick in the large mirror near the sinks and thoroughly approved of her reflection. The result was perfect. A fifteen-year-old fashionista.

She walked along until she hit the main road on Deansgate and got a few complimentary beeps from passing cars which made her feel good. It was quite a way but eventually she crossed over to Quay Street and sashayed down to Granada TV Studios. There was already a huge throng of fans gathering at the front, side and back. She pulled a face because she wanted a clear view of John and Paul when they arrived. She pushed her way through, but she was lost in the crowd.

This isn't good. I won't be able to see them properly. Becca, put on your thinking cap!

She returned to the front of the building where several wide steps led up to the glass-fronted reception area. She noticed the uniformed door attendant sat at his desk looking very official, but he was annoyingly in her way. Then she had a brilliant flash of inspiration. It was worth a try. She walked through the doors, straight up to the commissionaire, as if she had been invited. He got up from his seat when he saw her coming towards him.

"You're not allowed in here," he stipulated.

"Well, you see, I am expected."

"What's your name?"

"Becca Beacon. My brother Mikey has a friend who works for you. He's one of the cameramen and he promised to give me a tour of the studios. I have to be honest with you, I've deliberately chosen today because I knew that John Lennon and Paul McCartney would be filming here," she lied, with an irresistible wide smile.

"Let me see if you're on the list."

"Oh, I don't think I will be. I'm not a guest as such."

"What's the name of the cameraman?" he asked with a sceptical expression.

"Jeff Brett."

"Hmm. Just stay where you are while I check that out."

"Of course."

He went back to his seat, and at the same time the actress Pat Phoenix, who played Elsie Tanner in *Coronation Street*, walked through the door. Becca recognised her instantly. She was very glamorous and looked as if she owned the studio.

"Good morning, Albert," she said warmly, glancing briefly at Becca.

"Good morning, Miss Phoenix. Can I get you anything before you start rehearsals?" he asked reverently.

He was engaged in conversation when Becca took advantage of the situation. She sidled towards another set of stairs, which would take her into the main building. They were still chatting as she casually disappeared out of sight.

She found herself in a maze of different rooms, offices, and television sets. Becca was in awe of her surroundings. Although it was crammed full of staff and crew, nobody took any notice of her. They presumed she was part of the set-up, so she could explore without trepidation. Her head was full of The Beatles and their past performances.

My God, to think they were here for their appearance in 1962! I wonder which studio it was filmed in? I remember sitting on the carpet in front of the TV, my stomach in knots. I'd heard them on the radio, but I didn't know what they looked like. I was already hooked but when I saw them, my temperature soared through the roof. The day my world changed forever. Three years ago.

She bumped into Bamber Gascoigne, who was the presenter of University Challenge. He just smiled at her, so she grinned back. Then further along she saw some more of the *Coronation Street* cast. Then she literally collided with Johnnie Hamp, who had championed The Beatles on Granada TV in 1962, one year before they achieved national fame. He apologised for barging into her and then spoke to his associate.

"Now, this is going to be one hell of a great tribute to the Lennon-McCartney partnership. They've actually interrupted recording sessions for their next album to do this for us. We've got to make sure that all the scripted links between songs are perfect."

Becca's heart skipped several beats. *Oh, my word! I'm in the thick of it all. I'll just hang around until they arrive.*

Unfortunately, her elation was extremely short-lived, as she looked up to see the irate commissionaire, Albert, walking steadfastly towards her, wagging his index finger.

"Now then, young lady! You're here under false pretences and you're trespassing, so I want you to leave."

He grabbed her arm, propelling her down to the reception area, lecturing her on compliance every step of the way. Becca remained silent but deflated. Albert even accompanied her down the outdoor steps to make sure she was totally ousted.

"All right, all right, I'm going. Don't get your brass-buttoned jacket in a twist," she complained.

"You're a cheeky young madam. You're lucky I didn't call the police," he scolded.

"I only wanted to see John and Paul in the flesh. I've loved them since 1962. Your generation don't get it. You'll never understand!"

"Go and join all the screaming idiots outside the building. It's where you belong!"

Becca stuck out her tongue in a childish gesture. She was so frustrated to be back in the ever-increasing crowd of fanatics. They jostled her as she made her way between the hundreds of bodies gathered in anticipation of clapping eyes on John and Paul.

She managed to force her way through and walked round the side of the building where the long, glass-fronted corridor gave a full view of the interior. Suddenly she heard hysterical screams that nearly pierced her eardrums. She stood on tiptoes to see more clearly. And there they were. In all their Beatle glory. Her two icons behind the translucent wall. John was laughing at something, and Paul was talking to a producer. They stopped momentarily and waved to the fans outside. Becca thought her heart would cease to beat.

Oh, my God. They're only a short walk away from me! I can't believe it. Oh, why did that bloody doorman find me! I would have been in the building right now! Talk about bad timing! Just look at them! They're real. They're not posters on my wall. I want to cry, and I don't know why. That rhymes. Here I am! They call me Beatle girl. I love you both. So very much.

*

Becca was unaware that her form master had phoned her parents when she did not turn up for school. It was Shirley's day off and she was cleaning the kitchen floor when the telephone rang. She tutted as she left the job half-done and put the wet mop back in its bucket. She wiped her hands on an old tea towel and answered the call.

"Hello, Mrs. Shirley Beacon here."

"Hello, Mrs. Beacon. It's Mr. Dunn, Rebecca's teacher. I'm somewhat concerned that she's not in attendance today. We've heard nothing from yourself to explain her absence. Is she unwell?"

Shirley's heart skipped a beat and her mouth suddenly felt dry.

"She's not in school? But she left this morning as usual to catch the train!"

"Was she wearing her uniform?"

"Yes! Full regalia and carrying her sports bag."

"Sports bag?"

"She said she could put all her textbooks in it, along with her gymnastic romper and pumps."

"I see."

"Mr. Dunn, I'm really worried. Should I call the police? She's never done this before."

"You can report it, but they usually wait twenty-four hours to make sure that the person is missing. Is there anywhere you can think of that she could have gone to instead? I mean, did she have another journey in mind at all? It's not unusual for a pupil to abscond. Unfortunately, they don't realise the stress it can cause their family. Think carefully before you call the police."

"Knowing Rebecca, she would have mentioned her plans. It's a well-known fact that she's rebellious but I have to tell you, Mr. Dunn, that I'm truly worried."

"I'll let you know immediately if she arrives. In the meantime, have a think on where she might be today. There's a strong possibility she's playing truant, but I do understand your concern."

"Hopefully she'll just show up," replied Shirley, crossing her fingers.

"It's more than likely but I'll be in touch again."

Shirley put the phone back on its cradle and her heartbeat doubled with anxiety.

She climbed the stairs and entered Becca's bedroom. She was looking for clues and all her personal effects were in there. The Beatles pictures and posters dominated the walls. There were more than ever before, now encroaching on the actual ceiling. For once, Shirley looked at them with longing rather than disdain. After all, they were representational of Becca's presence and passion.

After routing around and finding nothing, Shirley opened the dressing table drawer. Inside there was some jewellery, a half-empty bottle of perfume, newspaper cuttings on the Fab Four, a spare brush and comb, a couple of different coloured lipsticks, a compact mirror, and John Lennon's latest book *A Spaniard in the Works.* She flicked through it and glanced at the nonsensical stories and drawings and tutted to herself. *What the heck she sees in him, God only knows.*

Then nestling underneath one of the articles, hiding in plain sight, she found Becca's diary. Shirley was a bit hesitant to read it because after all, it was personal, but the circumstances made her invade that privacy. She had no choice but to look inside at today's date. And there it was! An entry in bold letters for Monday 1st November 1965:

> *My gorgeous John and Paul are filming at Granada TV today and tomorrow. Hold on, you two dreamboats, because I'm on the way to meet you both. I'll be the one with the widest smile, wearing a denim jacket and mini-skirt, skinny-rib jumper and kitten-heel shoes. Your number one fan. They call me Beatle girl. You won't be able to miss me. See you soon. Love and kisses, Becca B. xxx*

Shirley felt relief and anger simultaneously. Then she was so incensed that she nearly ripped out the page. Her complexion turned bright red, and her blood pressure shot through the roof. She had to sit down on the bed and compose herself.

I might have known! Beatles! Beatles! Beatles! Rebecca, for God's sake! It's three years since this madness began. When will it stop? Will you ever buckle down and appreciate your privileged education? Yes, privileged! You won a scholarship and you're throwing it all away! Now I know why you took that sports bag instead of your briefcase. You had to change your clothes. Your school uniform was a definite no-no! What am I going to do about you?

She glowered at The Beatles posters and fixed her irate stare on John and Paul in particular.

"It's all your fault!" she said aloud. "Everything was fine until she clapped eyes on you two! Especially you, John Lennon!"

She went back downstairs and telephoned the school. She was not certain of what she was going to say to the teacher, but she had to find some excuse for getting her daughter off the hook.

"May I speak to Mr. Dunn, please. I'm Mrs. Shirley Beacon, Rebecca Beacon's mother."

She waited with bated breath until he took her call.

"Yes, hello, Mrs. Beacon. Have you any further news?"

"Well, actually I have. She's… well apparently, she was feeling rather unwell and stopped off at her aunt's house. She didn't want to worry me. She knows it was wrong of her, but she thought she might have felt better and been able to go to school a bit later. But she's really under the weather. I'm very sorry about this. If she had told me from the start, I would have just kept her at home," lied Shirley to protect Becca from possible expulsion, should they know the real story.

"Oh, I see. Well, I hope she feels better soon."

"I'll keep you informed. Thank you for your understanding. It's much appreciated."

"No problem. I'm glad she's safe."

Shirley put the phone down and made herself a strong cup of tea. She looked at her watch. It was one o'clock, so another three hours to go before Becca would come home. She wondered what she was doing right now and what lies she would concoct about her day.

She's with all the other lunatic fans! Anything could happen to her in that crowd. And for what? A glimpse of the so-called Mozarts of the twentieth century? Her dad's bought her a ticket for their concert next month. Couldn't she have waited until then? Why did she have to go creeping around with a bag full of Mary Quant clothes? Has she played truant with a few other girls? Did she go round to one of their houses first? Has she put full make-up on, including her Dusty Springfield eyes? She doesn't need all that muck on her face. Oh, God. Wait until Eric hears about this. He won't like it one little bit. This is one time when he'll find it hard to defend her. She's taking it to the limit and playing him like a puppet on a string. But even a worm turns.

*

Becca had walked around town nearly all day. She did a fair bit of window shopping and then popped into Lewis's music department where she could stand in a record booth and listen to the song of her choice. She'd asked to hear their latest single, 'Day Tripper', but they did not have it in stock as the release date was not until the 3rd December, along with their sixth studio LP, 'Rubber Soul'.

So, she'd plumped for 'Help' and the flip side 'I'm Down' on the pretext of purchasing it.

"Do you know that John Lennon and Paul McCartney are in Manchester today?" the assistant had asked her with a toothy grin. "That's why we're not as busy as usual."

"I believe so." *Go away. I'm upset enough without your daft questions.*

"Are you a fan?"

"You could say that." *Why don't you take a long walk off a short pier?*

"There's still plenty of time to see them. They're at Granada TV. Apparently, the crowds are enormous. They've got to come out sooner or later."

"I just want to listen to their record. Both sides."

"Well, it's not often they're here. A true fan would want to be as close as possible."

"And a true shop assistant would listen to this customer's request and not annoy her."

"I'm only trying to help. There's no need to be so rude."

"I'm not rude, I'm just honest. So, please can I hear their record?"

He snorted slightly as he nodded his head. She entered the booth and waited for the song to begin.

As usual she felt a surge of overwhelming happiness and excitement at the sound of their voices. It truly was a panacea that touched her heart and spirit. She bathed in the magical, musical moment and all the previous frustration on missing out on their actual presence melted away, and was replaced by the ecstatic realization that she would be seeing them in concert next month.

As she left the booth, the assistant asked her if she

wanted to buy the single. He was dressed like a Beatle but looked more like Jerry Lewis in *The Nutty Professor.*

"I've already got it. I just wanted to hear it for the millionth time. Bye for now."

"Well, really!" he exclaimed as she walked away, raising her arm, and waving her hand in the air, with her back towards him.

She looked at her watch and thought it was time to go home. She had not eaten since breakfast and felt very hungry. She made her way to Victoria train station and got changed into her school uniform in the washroom. She removed every scrap of make-up off her face.

Mum will never know about today. It was a damp squid in the end, but I did see them, even if it was through a glass wall. Oh, that bloody sergeant major of a doorman! I was literally five minutes away from a face-to-face unforgettable moment. What would I have said to them? I'll never know.

*

Shirley was waiting impatiently for Becca's return. At four-fifteen she let herself in with her key, as her mother came into the hallway at the same time.

"Hi, Mum. Tell you what, I'm really starving. May I have something to eat early, please? The school meals are getting worse. I left it all."

"Really?"

"Well today it was rubbish. Fish pie with vegetables. The mash tasted like wallpaper paste and the fish were swimming all over the plate. The pudding was supposed to be rhubarb and custard. It was anything but, and I hate it at the best of times. It looked like an action painting," she lied magnificently.

"What about the lessons? Were they just as bad?"

"They're always bad, so why should today be any different?"

"Why indeed."

"Anyway, I'll just pop upstairs and get out of my uniform. I want to be comfy."

"Just a minute, young lady!" instructed Shirley, in a tone that made Becca suspicious.

"What?"

"Give me your sports bag."

"Why?"

"Just hand it over. Your romper needs washing, and your pumps will need whitening."

"Oh, that's OK. I can wear them again. They're not that bad."

"Oh, aren't they?"

"No. Mum, you look upset. What's wrong?"

"What's wrong? What's wrong! I'll tell you what's bloody well wrong!" swore Shirley. "Three insufferable words! The bloody Beatles!"

Becca was taken aback at the fierce expression on her mother's pretty face. Her green eyes darkened and changed colour.

"Your form master rang to say that you'd not turned up! I was worried sick, so I had no choice but to look for a clue in your bedroom. I found your diary in the drawer. Do you get the picture, Rebecca Beatle-barmy Beacon? Do you?"

"Mum—"

"Don't 'Mum' me! Anything could have happened today! You bunk off school! You get changed into an outfit that's far too outrageous for your own safety! You were presumably in the middle of a hysterical crowd of brainwashed teenagers, trying to get near the two bad influencers! Those rock 'n' roll rabble rousers who have taken over the world and caused more unrest and anarchy than any other musical group in history! It's a disease! An untreatable disease! I'm so angry with you!"

"It could have been worse. I might have gone tomorrow instead. George and Ringo are joining them. Today it was mostly other artists covering their songs. So, the next day would have been the *four* rabble rousers and even more fans. At least I chose the less-crowded day."

"What do you want? A medal? I give up, Becca. I've a good mind to stop you going to that concert next month!"

"No way! I've waited three years to see them sing live! Three whole years and a bit! I'll leave home altogether if I can't go to the show! Mum, please! It will break my heart in two if I don't go! It really will," she pleaded, with tears brimming over in her appealing brown eyes.

"You must promise me this, Becca. Don't you dare to do anything so reckless *ever* again! I had to lie to your teacher and say that you were unwell. Your bloody Beatles have made me a liar by proxy!"

"I'm so sorry, Mum. I promise, I truly promise you that I'll always tell you what I'm doing. Really, I will," she pleaded, with her fingers crossed in her blazer pocket.

Shirley looked her directly in the eyes and relented. "Right then, get changed. I'm too worn out from worrying.

I've decided not to tell your dad. He'll go mad and I can't take any more stress."

"Aw, Mum. I really am sorry. Is it OK to have my dinner earlier? I'm so hungry. Pretty please?"

"Years ago, you would have gone to bed with bread and water if you'd misbehaved!"

"But this is 1965 and I'm your one and only, totally unique daughter. So, chips, eggs and baked beans would be very acceptable," she said charmingly, buttering Shirley up and kissing her repeatedly on the cheek. "I can always sing for my supper if you like, and it won't be a Beatles song."

"Enough! Don't push your luck! Now, let's draw a line under all of this."

"Yes, Mummy," she agreed, double-crossing her eyes and pulling a funny face.

Shirley shook her head and sighed.

"Go upstairs. I'll peel some potatoes and get your chips ready."

"Mum, I just want to hear a few songs from their latest LP. I'll keep the volume down while I get changed. You don't mind, do you?"

"You've got a right cheek."

"Well, I thought I'd be more considerate and ask you if it was OK."

"If you were more thoughtful you wouldn't be asking me at all, after what I've been through today. I got such a shock when Mr. Dunn rang. I thought something really bad had happened to you."

"It did. I was on the verge of meeting them when the commissionaire at Granada threw me out."

"What do you mean he threw you out?"

"I got into the building while he was busy talking to Pat Phoenix. He didn't see me go up the stairs. I walked around the studios. Mum, it was so thrilling. Just knowing that my icons were going to arrive at any minute. My heart was in my mouth."

"But you were trespassing. It was wrong."

"I was being adventurous. It was such a buzz until that uniformed, public nuisance found me. Another five minutes and I would have come face to face with John and Paul."

Shirley was speechless but her thoughts were active. *What can any of us do? She's just our Becca. I don't know who she takes after. I'm so relieved that she's safe. She's one on her own all right! Dearie me. Where's the chip pan? Bloody Beatles!*

Chapter Six

Tuesday, 7th December 1965 is a date that will live forever in Becca's Beatle-crazy head. Manchester was covered in thick fog when the band finally arrived, later than scheduled.

It began as another ordinary school day but there was nothing standard about her emotions before the show. Becca sat through the lessons with her stomach in knots as the anticipation of the evening's entertainment became unbearable. The teachers were lecturing to the classroom walls because absolutely nothing registered in her mind except her magnificent obsession.

Her friends Jane, Lynne, and Sally were also on tenterhooks, their concentration waning rapidly in view of the fact that they were accompanying Becca to the concert. It was Becca's father, Eric, who had actually obtained three extra tickets for them, and they had gladly reimbursed him.

In the lunchbreak, the four of them sat together in the refectory, just pushing the food around their plates. They were in a state of high excitement and had lost their appetites completely. Becca stared out of the window and noticed that the fog was denser than before.

"I hope the weather improves before tonight," she observed with a frown.

"I feel sick," groaned Jane. "My nerves are all over the place. The thought of seeing them is just too much."

"As you know, my mum's asked us back for tea. She feels it's best if we all go together. I think she's right," affirmed Becca.

"I hope she won't get upset if I leave the food."

"You're not on your own, Jane. My insides are looping the loop. I've been on the toilet all morning. It's stomach churning," agreed Lynne.

"What if they stop the trains and buses?" asked Sally. "The fog is really thick."

"They won't. We've had other days like this before. Anyway, my dad will drive us there if he has to."

"I feel sick," reiterated Jane.

"Have some sponge pudding. It's your favourite. We've got to eat something otherwise we'll all pass out," advised Becca.

"I'll faint anyway, the minute they walk on stage," sighed Lynne.

"You better not! You can't miss the eighth wonder of the world!"

"Oh, Becca! Can you believe it? The Beatles are in Manchester! They're here and we're going to be with them in the same room! In *exactly* the same room! Help!"

After lunch they had a maths lesson. Mr. Jones was his usual miserable, saturnine self, especially when he looked in Becca's direction. He was lecturing on geometry and going into great detail about the properties of space, such as the distance, shape, size and relative position of figures. It all went over Becca's Beatle-blocked head. *I wish he'd go on holiday in an ocean liner and get shipwrecked!*

Later on, she had PE. In a way it was a welcome release as she leaped over the vaulting horse and landed beautifully on the other side. She felt a rush of adrenaline. Her handstands and cartwheels were perfectly executed. Then she proceeded to climb the ropes right to the top and was praised by Miss Collins, her gym teacher, for the skills she had shown. As she slid downward, she had a vision of John and Paul. In her vivid imagination she was conversing with them.

Hi Johnny, I've waited so long to see you in real life. I'm your kindred spirit and I know how you think. I just do. You're so gifted and one of the sexiest singers I've ever seen. I love your face and voice. It's so... well, it's so... John. As for you, Pauly, you look like a matinee idol. Do you pluck your eyebrows? Because they're more arched than mine! I love your face and voice, too. You're a first-class dreamboat. I think you and John are the best songwriters of the twentieth century.

For a moment she nearly let go of the rope, so deep was her contemplation. She held on for dear life and coasted down until she landed on solid ground. *Oops, that was close. Concentrate, Becca. I nearly fell. I don't want any broken bones! Or to go to the wrong kind of theatre!*

The last lesson of the afternoon was English language.

Although she was pretty adept at punctuation and grammar, her focus was in short supply. She looked over at her friends and they had the same otherworldly expressions. All of them were on Planet Beatles and nothing resonated apart from tonight's entertainment.

Quite a number of the other pupils were also going to the concert. There was something spiritual in the air and they were all tuned into the ethereal wavelength. Becca had a psychic connection with her icons. Sometimes she knew what was going to happen without being told, so her thoughts became an actuality. It was exciting and unsettling simultaneously. When she looked at John in particular, she felt an indefinable, strong feeling about his welfare. She still believed that there was a battlefield of emotion and intensity going on inside his head. She understood because she was very similar. All of her circle thought she was being dramatic, but she knew that it was intuition and not a figment of her vivid imagination.

The school bell rang and it was time to leave. The four of them walked along the route to the train station in thick fog.

"Oh, bloody hell! What if they cancel the show?" moaned Lynne.

"They won't, so think positive!" replied Becca, but inside she was quaking with the possibility that Lynne could be right.

"Well, the trains are still running," observed Jane, as one arrived through the tunnel. They raced down the stone steps, dragging their cases behind them, practically falling over in the process. They plonked themselves down on seats in the carriage, breathless from rushing and the thought of tonight's extravaganza. When they were settled, they chatted about the evening.

"I wonder what songs they'll sing?" questioned Lynne.

"Probably a mixture of old and new," replied Sally.

"I don't think we'll hear much. The screams will drown out the sound," predicted Jane.

"I'm not going to scream," announced Becca, and they looked at her disbelievingly.

"Not much!" they said in perfect agreement.

"I won't. I promised John."

"What are you talking about? We'll go crazy the minute they walk on stage. What do you mean that you promised John?" puzzled Lynne.

"Just that! I spoke to his photo on my wall, and I've got this strong feeling that he's getting sick of it."

"If he was sick of it he wouldn't still be touring, and anyway, even if you don't scream it won't make any difference at all to the noise."

"Maybe, maybe not."

"You're kidding yourself, Becca!"

"Hmm. You're probably right. I won't scream, I'll just spontaneously combust!"

The four of them laughed out loud. There were a few passengers nearby that tutted. Then a woman in a ridiculous hat, that resembled a squashed mushroom on her head, actually looked Becca in the eye and spoke to her.

"I hate The Beatles and I hope that the fog keeps them well away!"

"Excuse me?"

"You heard me! My next-door neighbour's son plays their records from morning until night. Mainly after school in the evenings, at weekends, and all through the ruddy holidays! It's that bad that I feel like moving house! He's no consideration for anyone else! The Beatles don't sing! They shriek! Call that music? It's torture!"

"Have you got a piece of paper?" questioned Becca.

"Why?"

"Because I'll write down my telephone number and you can get in touch with my mother. You'd get on very well," she mocked.

"You're obviously one of those lunatics that go crazy at their so-called concerts."

"Oh, it's not just me. There's my three friends here plus the rest of the world, Mrs. Killjoy."

"You cheeky young madam."

"I've only confirmed your opinion. Anyway, the next stop is ours. You'll be relieved to hear that the crazy lunatics are going to get off the train. So, you'll be able to keep yourself company. That will be so boring for you."

"Well, I never! Good manners cost nothing!"

"Then *you'll* have lots of money, won't you?"

"Oh! Such cheek!"

"Give us a kiss," replied Becca, in John Lennon-mode.

They all giggled as they got off the train. The woman in the toadstool hat waved her fist at them through the window. They returned the gesture in unison.

"Oh, bother! I can hardly breathe in this smog. It's getting worse by the second," moaned Lynne.

"She's right you know, Becca," agreed Jane, wrapping her scarf around her mouth.

"Don't be so negative. Everything will be OK."

"I'm not being negative. I'm being practical. This

is a pea-souper! I can't see anything in front of me," complained Lynne.

"We'll get there somehow. Stop worrying."

*

Shirley was waiting anxiously for them in the porch. She frowned deeply as she checked the visibility outside. She could not see a thing through the dense fog. *It's bad enough they're going to the hysterical concert. Surely it will cancelled? Even the mopheads might not arrive at the theatre. That would make my year.*

She heard voices and the four of them came into view as they walked up the driveway. It was as if they had materialised from another time and place.

"Hi, Mum. Everyone's here. We're not that hungry, so don't get upset if we only want small portions," explained Becca.

"I'm not that hungry, either. It's bad enough that Mikey's going with his friends. I wish he was leaving from home, rather than Alan's house. At least that way you could have gone with him. I'm worried sick about the weather." Shirley frowned deeply.

"Well, the trains are still running and there's four of us travelling there together. It's not as if I'm going alone."

They all entered the house, glad to shut the door on the ever-increasing smog. The table was set beautifully but nobody really noticed. Shirley had made vegetable soup, followed by a chicken casserole that smelled delicious.

"Put your cases down and you can all get changed

after you've eaten," she suggested. "I hope you've brought sensible clothes."

They all looked at each other. There was not one practical outfit amongst them. It was a case of fashion over fuddy-duddy clobber.

"Now take your coats off and come and sit at the table. A bowl of steaming hot soup will go down a treat on a night like this."

"Where's Dad?" asked Becca.

"He's not home from work yet. He phoned to say he'll be late because he has loads of paperwork to do. I'm concerned how he's going to drive home in this freezing, thick fog."

They took their places and actually enjoyed the soup with a bread roll. It went down smoothly and warmed them up. Shirley came in with an enormous oven dish full to the brim of chicken and vegetables. Although it looked and smelled appetising, they did not do justice to its contents.

"Oh, come on girls, you've only had a mouthful or two. Try a little bit more, please," encouraged Shirley.

"I couldn't possibly, Mrs. Beacon. It's all very lovely but I feel sick with nerves. The soup was ideal and like a meal in a bowl," explained Jane.

"Yes. I feel the same," agreed Lynne.

"Me too," added Sally.

"What about you, Becca? Or is that a silly question?"

Becca was in Beatle-dreaming posture and did not respond. She was gazing into space, her mind whirling with imaginative scenarios.

"Becca, I'm talking to you. Would you like some chicken casserole?"

In her vivid imagination Becca was storming the stage towards John and Paul. It did not matter which one she reached first as long as she completed the task.

"Becca!" reiterated her mother, and she snapped out of her trance.

"Yes, Mum?"

"For the umpteenth time, do you want some casserole?"

"Oh, thanks, but no thanks. I couldn't possibly. I feel full from the soup. It was really tasty," she replied, glassy-eyed and totally distracted.

"I don't know. It's as if you're all under a witch's spell. A Beatle-hypnosis. I'll never understand what's so special about them."

"They're magical. Always were and always will be," fawned Becca.

They made their way upstairs into Becca's bedroom and got changed in front of her Beatles gallery of pictures. The girls wore similar clothing of skinny-rib jumpers, hipster trousers and Chelsea boots. They put make-up on in the dressing table mirror, jostling each other for a clearer view.

"We should be warm enough wearing our coats over the outfits. I'll fasten mine before my mother does a spot-check on what's underneath."

Becca's jumper was so skimpy that her bare midriff was on display, especially with her trousers resting low down on her hips. Her eyes looked huge with lashings of mascara and grey shadow on the lids. Panstick foundation and frosted pink lipstick completed the look. She was positively glowing with joy and anticipation.

"You look so cool, Becca," flattered Jane.

"So do you. We're all Beatle girls tonight! Oh, my God, my heart is beating so fast. I've waited so long for this. Nothing's going to get in the way. So, let's go!"

Shirley had grave misgivings as they set off to the local railway station, arm in arm, through the dense fog. They all wore the latest faux fur black hats, which kept their heads and ears warm. Their scarves were wrapped around their mouths for protection.

"Come right back if the trains are cancelled!" shouted Shirley, but their minds were on just one thing. The Beatles. The Fab Four. The biggest group worldwide.

There was a large throng of people waiting for a train, most of them going to the show. When one appeared they all cheered and scrambled for a seat. All the way to Victoria station, the whole conversation was John, Paul, George and Ringo. It seemed the carriage was full of Beatle fans. At the terminus the crowds were heaving. Then there was an announcement over the loudspeaker informing everyone that all further transport had been cancelled, including the buses.

"We'll just have to walk to the ABC Cinema," coughed Becca, the fog seeping into her lungs.

"But we'd normally get a bus. It's quite a long way. Especially in this stupid fog. I can't see a damn thing and I'm not even sure which direction to take, even in broad daylight," complained Jane.

"We'll just follow the crowd. They're in the same boat," observed Becca.

"Good idea," mumbled Lynne behind her scarf.

Everybody formed an endless queue and stuck like glue to the person directly in front of them. It resembled a never-ending Conga without the dance steps. People were singing Beatle songs to keep their spirits alive and kicking. Becca felt she was in a science fiction film. Voices were filtering through from another dimension with no visible human beings.

Nobody was really sure that The Beatles would arrive on time, but it did not stop their enthusiasm for the occasion. After a long walk, they finally reached their destination. The enormity of the event really kicked in as they queued up, tickets in hand and hearts pounding ridiculously fast.

"Are The Beatles here? Did they make it through the fog?" Becca asked the doorman.

"Just about. They were wearing smog masks," he replied, with a look of great relief on his weather-beaten face.

"Are they OK to perform?" questioned Jane, with a frown.

"Absolutely. They're consummate professionals. The show must go on. Don't worry, they're setting up the sound equipment as we speak."

A great cheer resounded through the crowd. Some fans burst into tears because they had been worried all day about the consequences of the weather on the concert. Becca's entourage all looked emotional and hugged each other with relief.

"They're here, Becca! They're here!" expounded Jane.

"*We're* here! I wasn't too sure deep down if we'd make it! Hallelujah!"

Once inside the theatre they each bought a programme and then found their seats. They were in the stalls, ten rows back from the front, and had a great view of the stage. Coats, scarves, hats and bags were withdrawn, and they sat down, full of anticipation. For some reason, Becca forgot to take off her hat. She was so excited that she did not realise it was still on her head. Her friends were far too worked up to even notice.

The place was filling up rapidly. It was jam-packed, both downstairs and in the gallery. Bodies were already draped over the balcony in readiness for the incredible event. The Beatles were top of the bill, but before their act there were several artists who would perform. It was more like a variety show, with their icons headlining the whole production.

The compere, Jerry Stevens, appeared on stage. He introduced the acts one by one, comprising of The Paramounts, Beryl Marsden, The Koobas, The Marionettes and The Moody Blues. Becca particularly liked the latter and their single 'Go Now'. They reproduced it perfectly. Denny Laine was her favourite member of the band on guitar and lead vocals.

The anticipation was becoming unbearable, and she could feel the tension filtering through the whole auditorium. Becca was sticky with expectation because she knew that the next act would be her icons.

Oh come on! I can't bear it any longer! I've waited three years for this! Please!

As if to answer her thoughts, the penultimate act finished their set, the audience applauded, and Jerry Stevens came back on stage.

"And *now*! And *now*! Yes *now*! We have the moment you've *all* been waiting for! The moment you will remember *forever*! They were here in 1963 and *now they're back*!

The screams were audible even before they appeared. Just the build-up to their spot was enough to set the theatre alight with unrestrained Beatlemania.

"Are you ready for this?"

The screams became even louder and prolonged. Becca and her friends were on their feet.

"Are you sure you're all ready?" he repeated, whipping up the hysteria.

Becca thought she would die from the suspense. The presenter could hardly be heard above the noise of the crowd.

"OK! We are honoured to welcome for one night only, the absolutely incredible, fantastic and amazing Fab Four! They're only behind the curtain! Do you want to see them? Do you want to hear them?"

The atmosphere descended into sheer lunacy and that was without a Beatle in sight.

"OK! No more waiting! We've rolled out the red carpet for musical royalty. So here they are! Let's hear it for the biggest band in the world today! *Welcome to Manchester*! *The Beatles*!"

The curtain went up and there they were, large as life and looking out of this world. They went straight into 'She's A Woman' with Paul singing the lead vocal. Rays of light danced upon their faces and revealed their identical attire of dark suits and impressive guitars. Ringo's raised drumkit towered at the back. John, Paul and George stood at the front, in a sexy line, microphones at the ready. They all looked incredible.

Becca forgot her pledge to John and screamed so loud that she thought she was going to be sick. Jane just stood frozen to the spot, with every finger stuck in her mouth. Lynne and Sally were hugging each other with the intense emotion of it all.

The heat was on. Their music should have shattered the sound barrier but instead it was brutally destroyed among a deafening crescendo of screams and hysteria. Bodies hurled themselves at the stage like an invasion of belligerent meteorites. Fans hung over the balcony, dishevelled and unkempt, resembling a wild display of rag doll merchandise. Some yelled and clapped with a crazy fever, the perspiration running down their faces. The theatre was a factory of human machinery and seemed to rotate on an axis of ceaseless adulation. All Becca could see, hear, feel, know, want and desire, was expressed in an insane exhibition that drained her of mind and reason, and stripped her of self-control and femininity.

Right the way through George's 'If I Needed Someone' and then Ringo's 'Act Naturally', the place was still erupting. Then John spoke and joked with the audience. Becca swooned and the screams around her were deafening as he launched into 'Nowhere Man'. After that, Paul introduced 'Baby's in Black' and the crowd went absolutely wild when he and John vocalised, eyeball-to-eyeball, through the same microphone. Just when she thought it could not get any better, John sang the lead vocal on 'Help!' with Paul and George harmonising beautifully in the background.

Becca did not realise that she was plucking clumps of faux fur out of her hat. The only consolation would be that it was not her actual hair! Her headgear looked as if it had alopecia. Large quantities of synthetic fur were missing, leaving bald patches here and there.

John sat at the keyboard for 'We Can Work It Out'. Paul, once again, was the lead vocalist and John harmonised with him in the middle of the song. Becca began to cry. The mascara circled around her eyes and cascaded down her face. She looked like a certifiable panda. All around her the fans were sobbing, screaming, standing, shouting, yelling and waving. Then Paul sang 'Yesterday' on his own. The screams drowned out his vocals. Becca was so moved by his rendition she wanted to shut everyone up, so that she could bathe in the beauty of the composition.

The penultimate song was their latest single 'Day Tripper'. Again, it effectuated a Beatle circus of mass hysteria. All too soon they performed their last number 'I'm Down'. John sat at the keyboard once more, as Paul belted out the number in his inimitable style. When John used his elbow to run up and down the keys, in the middle of the song, something inside Becca exploded on a subliminal level.

She sprinted down the aisle to the front of the stage. She found herself clambering on to the podium in order to reach him but was pulled back unceremoniously by the seam of her trousers. A burly bouncer ripped the seam wide open with brute strength, but Becca was not aware of the damage. Only the fact that she was stopped from attaining her ultimate goal. She stayed where she was and had a fantastic view of the four of them at close quarters. They looked stunning. She was so close to them and yet so far away. She wanted to be with them and express all the emotions that were swirling around her head and body.

She wished she could tell them about the childhood abuse and her clueless teachers, but more so, to explain how instrumental they had been in saving her sanity. She wanted to sing them her parodies and talk about her desire to write her own songs one day. She wanted to tell John that she knew how he ticked, that she had a spiritual link with him, regardless of her tender years. But it was not to be. It was just a very vivid fantasy.

When the last strains of their exhausting performance died away, they thanked the audience and then abandoned the stage, leaving the theatre to resemble the aftermath of a rampaging storm. It was as if a violent rotation of air had been in contact with the surface of the earth. Becca did not really understand what incited such an unbearable emotion. No human beings could possibly be worthy of such inordinate or incredulous worship. Could they?

"I'm drained," croaked Jane, "but in seventh heaven."

"They were amazing! I can't believe it! I just love them more than ever!" raved Lynne.

"Sex on legs. That's what they all are. Sex on eight bloody legs!" exclaimed Sally.

"Where's Becca?" queried Jane when she saw that her seat was empty. "She's not left without us, has she?"

"I don't know. Maybe she's gone to the toilet or something."

They all looked around the theatre, which was half-empty. Then they saw her leaning against the podium looking absolutely bereft.

"I'll go," said Jane. "You two stay here with our coats and bags."

Jane approached her. Becca was crying and all her make-up had run down her face. Her hat was practically bald, and unbeknown to both of them, the back of her trousers were torn.

"Oh, Becca. What have you done to your hat? It's in shreds. Oh, please don't cry. They were wonderful. You should be jumping through hoops. Your dream came true after three years of waiting to see them," she said emotionally, putting a protective arm around her shoulder.

"I love them. I always will," sobbed Becca. "They've saved me from such torment. None of you really know."

"Know what? What are you saying?"

"I can't tell you, but just believe me that they helped me cope through such a shitty time."

Jane frowned as she saw the anguish in Becca's expression.

"Come with me. Lynne and Sally are waiting for us. I don't know how we're going to get back. There's no public transport. Let's go and find a café or something and have a cup of tea. My mouth is so dry and my throat hurts."

They returned to their seats and put on their coats, scarves and hats. Becca did not care that her hat looked like a plucked, flattened busby. Bags slung over their shoulders, they made their way out of the theatre into a formidable blanket of thick fog.

"It's even worse. How the hell are we going to get home?" groaned Sally. "I can't breathe in this smog, let alone walk in it."

"I need to find a phone box and call my dad," coughed Lynne.

Her father was a policeman, and he was on duty. If she could contact him at his station, he could somehow rescue them from their plight.

They found a nearby café and tumbled through the door into cleaner air. There was a spare table near the jukebox. They sat down and ordered four cups of tea with some scones. Becca went to the washroom and repaired her face in the mirror. She also removed her hat and brushed her flattened hair into a reasonable style. She came back into the room looking somewhat presentable and joined her friends. They took off their coats and tucked into their tea and scones, chatting away about the whole experience. All of them had husky voices from screaming.

"Wasn't John amazing playing 'I'm Down'? I really lost it when he elbowed his way across the keyboard. I just ran down to the front of the stage. I climbed up but 'The Incredible Hulk' pulled me back. I was only a few feet away from John. He's so dynamic! And so, so sexy!"

"So that's why you were out of your seat. We were all so hysterical that we didn't notice," verified Jane.

"I just stayed where I was and watched them all. They're even more stunning in the flesh. So striking and good-looking. Four magical, musical mannequins. I feel honoured to have been so close to them. It's probably the nearest I'll ever get to my fantasy. I'll never forget it. As long as I live."

"I won't forget it either," agreed Jane.

"Or me," sighed Lynne.

"Or me," repeated Sally.

"Hey, why don't we play a Beatle record on the jukebox?" enthused Becca, already getting out of her chair. "Look! 'I'm Down' is on the list. We can dance to it!"

They agreed enthusiastically and clubbed together for the three shillings charge to play the record of their choice.

The rhythm of the song was ideal for dancing. Becca got into the groove and stood on the spot, bending both arms backwards, as if she was rowing a boat, and lifting her legs in unison to the beat. She was so enthusiastic that the rest of the customers all clapped.

Her bare midriff was on show and, unbeknown to her, the split on the seam at the back of her trousers became even wider as she gyrated across the floor. One man leant to the side to have a closer look, and another cheered as if his football team had scored a goal.

"Oh, my God!" exclaimed Jane. "Just look at Becca's trousers at the back! They're ripped!"

Jane tried to get her attention, gesticulating and pointing wildly to alert her to the problem, but Becca was in her element and just waved back at her, thinking she was the bee's knees of dance. Jane got up and walked over to her.

"Come on! Dance with me!" exclaimed Becca, pulling her nearer.

"You've torn your hipsters and you can see your bloody knickers!"

"What?"

"I said, everyone can see your knickers! Your trousers are wide open at the back!"

The music was too loud, and Becca could not hear properly.

"What you say?"

"You've torn your trousers near your bum and you can see your navy blue knickers!" shouted Jane, but the record had finished, and all the customers heard every word.

Becca moved her hand over the damage and stood routed to the spot. She wanted to die of embarrassment.

She was even more mortified over the fact that she had her school knickers on, and not something more fashionable. *Bugger!*

"I thought it felt a bit draughty," she joked, trying to laugh it off. "It's that bouncer's fault for pulling me away. He should have let me storm the stage and kiss John and my knickers would still be intact. Oh heck, that sounds a bit racy, doesn't it?"

The whole room burst into laughter but that was Becca's intention. Her highly developed sense of the ridiculous came to the fore. She was in entertaining mode as she spoke to everyone.

"Anyway, I wanted to have another try to reach John and Paul. I nearly did. Then they could have sang 'Becca's in Blue' instead of 'Baby's in Black'. That would have made headlines in the Manchester Evening News! If P.J. Proby can do it on stage, then why can't I? He split his trousers from knee to crotch at the beginning of this year and was banned from every major theatre in Britain, not to mention the BBC and ITV channels. Good job I'm not famous!"

Everyone cheered and Becca took a bow. Inside she was still disconcerted but the actress in her came to the fore and nobody would ever have known. She ambled towards her seat with Jane, both hands behind her back, covering the open flap.

"Oh, Becca, you're a bloody scream," laughed Sally.

"Hilarious!" echoed Lynne.

"Joking apart, we need to work out a plan of getting back home. It's like a Hammer horror movie out there. I'm half expecting something diabolical to come out of the fog and swallow us up!"

"You're right, Becca. I have to find a phone box and call my dad. I know the number of the police station where he works," confirmed Lynne.

"Right, let's get going," she agreed.

They all waved goodbye to everyone, and Becca took an extra bow. Her coat covered her ripped trousers, and she wrapped her scarf around her mouth. She wore the semi-bald, faux-fur hat to keep her head warm. It looked ludicrous.

"What's your name darlin'?" asked a scruffy man with nicotine-stained teeth and a lewd grin.

"They call me Beatle girl. So tatty-bye for now."

"You need a new hat, luv."

"You need new teeth, luv."

They all laughed out loud as they walked into the street. The fog hit them straight away and even their scarves did not fully protect them. They coughed in unison and found a shop doorway close to the café. It was quite wide and under cover. They stopped to get their breath back.

"God, this is a nightmare. I think we should go back to the theatre and ask someone if there's a phone box nearby. If not, maybe they'll let us use their telephone. After all, it's an emergency of sorts," suggested Lynne.

"I'm just checking to see if I've put the programme in my bag," piped up Becca. "I'm not sure if I left it behind."

She searched through the contents and gave a sigh of relief when she found it and pulled it out to drool over the front cover that featured all four of her idols. Her friends suddenly screamed in unison.

"I know! You're all still back in the theatre, aren't you? Hey, this will be worth something one day. I'm keeping it forever with my ticket. It will be a reminder of the most amazing night of my life."

Becca looked up and realised her friends had gone. She was completely on her own, or so she thought. She shouted their names but there was no reply. *Oh, this is just great! Where the hell are they? Why didn't they wait for me?*

Out of the corner of her eye, to her right, she saw a human shape. The fog clouded her vision but then a man came into full view. He just stood there, in the doorway, with a psychotic grin on his spaced-out face. He moved even closer. She looked down and froze. *He's a bloody flasher! Oh, my God! No wonder they screamed! Thanks, girls, for deserting me. Keep calm, Becca. It's a phallus in the fog! That's a great title for a song! Oh bugger.*

She pushed him out of the way and ran for her life. She caught up with the others, five apertures down, where they were sheltering in shock.

"Thank you very much for your caring concern and support," she derided.

"We thought you were with us. We were just going to look for you," rasped Lynne.

"I bet."

"Oh, Becca. We couldn't believe what we were seeing. We just ran. I'm so sorry. Come here and give me a hug," implored Jane.

They all huddled together, not knowing whether to laugh or cry.

"Oh boy! This is turning out to be a night to remember in more ways than one. Trust us to meet Flash Gordon! It's a good job he couldn't see my knickers," joked Becca.

Her comment was the catalyst for the four of them to have hysterics. They burst into unrestrained laughter, splitting their sides with the absurdity of it all.

"Becca, you crack me up," chortled Jane.

After the laughter had died down, they decided to go back to the theatre. It would be virtually an impossible task to find a phone box, so Lynne wanted to ask permission to call her father from their phone. Fortuitously, the manager was in the foyer and after explaining their plight, he let her use the office telephone. She rubbed her cold hands together then rang Bootle Street Police Station and asked to speak to him.

"Hi, Dad. We're all stuck at the ABC because there's no buses or trains running. We can't walk too far in this fog anyway. Can you come and get us? Otherwise we'll be here all night," she explained.

"Stay where you are. I'll call for you, but it could be a while. I have to drive really slowly but I'll be there as soon as I can. Now stick together, OK?"

"OK, Dad. Thanks so much."

Lynne breathed a sigh of relief and informed the others. One hour later, her father rolled up in a police car. The four of them were shivering, coughing and feeling exhausted.

"I'll have to drive you back to the station first. I was in the middle of a meeting with the Chief Inspector. After that, I'll drop you off home, one by one."

Becca was so cold and breathless that she would have got into the car with Jack the Ripper as long as she could get home. When they arrived at Bootle Street, the sergeant gave them tea with some biscuits. They were cluttering up the entrance, so he led them to an empty cell. They sat on the floor, warming their hands around the cups and munching on the custard creams.

"My mum's always worrying about me getting into trouble. Wait 'til I tell her I supped tea in a prison cell. That'll go down well with my aunty Doreen. She'll be on her anti-Beatle soapbox forever. They both will."

The others just nodded and smiled. They were all drained from the events of the evening. They felt rather unwell and just needed a warm, cosy bed and a good night's sleep.

"It's school in the morning," Lynne reminded them. "Our cases and uniforms are still at Becca's, but I just want to sleep forever and dream of The Beatles. I need to forget all the rest."

By the time Lynne's father had finished his meeting and drove them to their houses, Becca did not put her key in the lock until well after midnight. She was the last one to be dropped off. Her mother and father were waiting up for her. When they heard the latch turn, they rushed into the hall to make sure she was all right. Shirley's mouth dropped open when she saw the state she was in.

"Just look at you! What have you done to your hat? The concert finished ages ago! Where have you been? Mikey got back OK. His friend gave him a lift. Why didn't you ask if you could come home with them? What happened? Becca! Answer me!"

"I don't feel well. I want to go to bed."

"*You* don't feel well! Neither do we! We've been worried sick!"

"Mum, we couldn't get back through the fog. Lynne's dad brought us home in his police car."

"Well, you should be used to that! Remember? When you were thirteen and broke into your school! A police car brought you home and they nearly arrested you for trespassing!"

"Shirley, enough now! She's safe! Becca, we've been out of our minds with worry."

"Dad, we really did try to find a phone box, but it was too foggy."

"So how did Lynne's father know where you all were?"

"They let her call him from the office in the theatre. He works at Bootle Street. He drove us there and we had to wait in a cell until he was ready to bring us home."

"A cell! You were in a prison cell!" gasped Shirley.

"Only until he was ready."

"Well, I hope it was all worth it! Those bloody Beatles! They'll see me off!"

"Give me your hat and coat and put your bag down," said Eric.

Becca was so tired she forgot about her outfit. Shirley went ballistic when she saw her bare midriff and torn trousers. Eric had to calm her down. He helped Becca up the stairs and into her bedroom. She was feeling rather weak, and her throat really hurt. He came back down to face the music.

Mikey was listening to Beatle records on his headphones and missed the commotion. When the track stopped playing, he heard his mother's raised voice. He realised that Becca had finally got home and wanted to make sure that she was all right.

"Is Becca back? I tried to spot her after the show but there were so many people that it was virtually impossible.

It was a miracle that Alan was able to drive me home in that fog."

Shirley was still ranting. "She comes home looking like something the cat's dragged in. I rue the day she ever set eyes on those deadbeats! She's uncontrollable. Like all their brainwashed female fans. Bloody Beatles!"

"Where is she?"

"Your father has helped her upstairs because she feels unwell."

"In what way?"

"Brain fog! Those roughnecks have a lot to answer for. She's under their spell and over the top."

"Seriously, Mum. She must be drained. The concert was amazing, and the reaction was off the scale. The weather caused chaos and Becca was stuck out there for ages trying to get home. She's probably caught a chill or something."

Eric appeared and went into the kitchen to boil the kettle. "She's shivering and I think she has a temperature. I'm going to make her a hot water bottle. Shirley, don't start. Where's the paracetamol? I've some left over from October when I had a bad cold."

"What about school?"

"What about school?" replied Eric.

"She won't be fit. The other three are probably in the same state. They've left their uniforms and cases here anyway."

Shirley was perfectly correct in her assumption. Becca and her friends all came down with heavy colds, hacking coughs and laryngitis. They were off school for a week. Shirley also had to take some time off work to look after her. Becca stayed in bed mostly and could only manage liquids. She lost quite a bit of weight. Shirley made endless trips up the stairs with drinks and soup.

"Well? Was it worth it, daughter of mine? I've been so worried about you," she said caringly, stroking Becca's fringe away from her eyes, and plumping up her cushions. "If I shout, it's only because I love you."

She half-smiled and held her mother's hand. "Love you, too," she whispered.

"Anyway, at least you've got the mopheads all around you for company. I've forgotten what colour paint the walls are!" she joked, observing the multiple posters and photographs.

Shirley left her sleeping. *When will the madness stop? It's an incurable disease! Bloody Beatles!* As for Becca, the closing of the year still saw her in the role of a stupefied slave to their undying influence.

Chapter Seven

George married model Patty Boyd on the 26th January 1966 at Epsom Register Office in Surrey. Becca was delighted for them both. They made a stunning couple.

As the year progressed, Becca felt a restlessness that was not easy to explain. Although she was always a thinker, she could still find pleasure in the smallest of things. On the outside she appeared her usual wacky self, but inside there was something on the boil. Her school syllabus was becoming really intricate and required a good deal of homework. Some nights she would actually concentrate on what she was given, if there was an interest in the subject. Then there were the times when she would scribble it all down the morning after, in the deserted cloakroom or caretaker's closet. She was not consistent at all.

By this time, her friends had buckled down to hard graft. A lot of them knew their future desires and needed a solid foundation to achieve them. Becca did not have a clue as to what she wanted to do, be, or achieve, with regards to her education. She loathed most of the subjects that they force-fed her, neither could she see any future with the ones she respected. Besides all that, there was a feeling deep down that she could not define. She was hardly the conventional schoolgirl that her teachers could praise. She was becoming aware of a painful loneliness. Not a loneliness for friendship or company, but a creeping awareness of life's essence through the eyes of a recruited realist.

Before this, she had a sheltered vision of everything, knowing she could have always crawled back to parental protection. If somebody stepped on her toes, she had her beloved Beatles to tell her fears to. But how long would she have either? Nothing was ever permanent. *What the heck is happening to me? Where's my fantasy Queendom? Those sandcastles in the air? I can't cope with this new way of thinking.*

If Becca was changing, it was of small comparison to The Beatles evolution. This was the year they began their highly creative climb, a time of cellos, orchestral sounds and experimentation, of collective individuality, and, more crucially, the end of their touring and the beginning of a classic recording revolution. Towards the closing of the year, they tossed their shaving tackle aside and began to grow facial hair. For most of the year they were slammed. So, as well as battling with her own problems, she now had to deal with the onslaught of insults directed against her infallible idols.

It started in March. John had given an interview and said that they were more popular than Jesus. The remark proved uncontroversial in the UK when the newspapers originally reported it. The New York Times largely ignored his quote. It was only when the comment was reprinted in a July issue of *Datebook*, an American teenagers' magazine with a political fringe, that it became notorious. Alabama radio hosts Tommy Charles and Doug Layton pilloried the comment as blasphemous and proposed a 'Ban The Beatles' crusade. They stopped playing all Beatles records. Numerous other hosts joined forces, even smashing the discs on air. This escalated even further, and some southern radio stations began to oversee mass burnings of their LPs. Even the Ku Klux Klan became caught up in it, nailing Beatle records to a cross before setting it alight.

Becca hit the roof when she read about the reaction. *He's entitled to his opinion. He wouldn't have said it if he thought it was going to cause such a hoo-hah. It was never initially criticised over here. It was only when those American religious fanatics whipped up all that poison that it became a vendetta. Their way of dealing with it was far worse than John's comment. They were violent and dangerous. I mean the Ku Klux Klan for a start! What? They're evil!*

Brian Epstein spoke up on John's behalf. He explained that John was certainly not comparing The Beatles to Jesus and that he was simply observing that The Beatles are, to many people, better known. Brian considered cancelling their US tour in case it put them in danger from the audiences. He even offered to cover the potential one million dollars loss himself. He extended the opportunity for US venues to cancel any upcoming appearances by the group. But none did.

When they got to Chicago in August, John held a press conference to apologise, even though he had not meant any harm. This brought about a good reaction and most of the anti-Beatles vehemence abated. Only a small number of religious demonstrators still threatened them.

The perception that such a well-loved group could be greeted with shocking dissention and ferocity, together with exhaustion after three years of Beatlemania, heralded a turning point in their lives. With the adaptation of a few live performances, The Beatles became a studio group from there onwards.

Before that decision, they had toured West Germany, Japan and the Philippines between the 24th June and the 24th July. The tour of America transpired from the 12th to the 29th August. Poor sound, exhaustion and unease about their security took its toll. They could never hear themselves play or sing because of the screaming.

Becca felt guilty for last year's reaction to their concert and 'spoke' to the pictures on her wall. "So sorry! I didn't mean to go hysterical. John. I promised you that I wouldn't scream but there was so much emotion inside me. I'd waited so long to see you all. I've known for a while that you're unhappy with the whole scene. Your song 'Help!' was literally how you felt. Sometimes I think you wish you were back in The Cavern. The early days. Without the pressure. I don't blame you. I understand. Fame on your scale is exhausting."

In the summer of 1966, on the 10th June, another single had been released: 'Paperback Writer' and the flip side 'Rain'. Then the single 'Yellow Submarine' coupled with 'Eleanor Rigby' together with their outstanding seventh studio album, 'Revolver', were all released on the 5th August.

Becca was also beginning to despise her surroundings. Nothing was sacred anymore. She wrote a poem to reflect her whirling thoughts.

Feelings were spoken they once were sublime
Connections are broken, cut off in their prime
Remind me to tell you your nectar is sour
The crust of your backbone is turning to flour
Your duties are labelled, your routine's your time
You're feeling unstable, your speech doesn't rhyme
Forget all the seaweed or marshmallow foam
Forget all the sunsets, or mountains to roam
Reject all the hillsides of mellowing hue
Disfigure the skylight of towering blue
Little Jack Horner's reloading his breath
He's mastered the pleasure of living his death.

*

Boyfriends had begun to feature in her life. She had quite a few dates with like-minded students but nothing serious. Her first crush, Terry Alexander, had moved to Scotland with his family. At first, she was somewhat upset, but then it was a case of out of sight, out of mind.

In August 1966 she was walking through Heaton Park with her friend Lynne. Two really good-looking guys approached them.

"Hi, my name's Ben," said the taller one. "What's yours?"

"Well, that would be telling," she flirted.

"Well, that's why I'm asking."

"Have a guess."

"I'm not psychic," he shot back.

"I am."

"Well then, what's my friend's name? Huh?" he teased.

"Well then, I'll have to consult my crystal ball. Just a minute. Oh dear, it's fallen into the lake! Drat it."

"You're a cheeky monkey, aren't you?" observed Ben, with a twinkle in his deep brown eyes.

"Actually, I'm a tiger, according to Chinese astrology."

"I'm Dave," said the other good-looker.

"I'm Lynne," shot back Becca's pal.

"Should we go for a drive? The car's only round the corner. We can have a coffee at the Espresso Bongo in town. We were going there anyway."

"Does the tiger want to come too?" asked Ben, with a smirk.

"After I've sharpened my claws," wisecracked Becca.

"Tell me your real name."

"Beatle girl."

"I should have known with a fringe that long."

"Her name's Becca and she's winding you up," laughed Lynne.

"Becca? Short for Rebecca, I presume?"

"You presume right."

"Right then, would you two lovely girls like to go on a date with us? We promise to behave," said Ben with a smile.

"Well, we don't really know you. Where are you from?" asked Lynne.

"We're home for the weekend but we're both students at Sheffield University."

"So how old are you?" enquired Lynne cautiously.

"I'm nineteen and Dave's twenty."

"We're only fifteen and still at school."

"That's OK. We'll treat you with the respect you deserve. Won't we, Dave?"

"Sure will."

"I'm sixteen next month," declared Becca.

"Sweet sixteen and never been kissed," joked Ben.

"That's debatable."

"So, let's go for a coffee and debate it."

They all laughed and although they had just met, Becca had an innate feeling she would be all right. On the surface it seemed risky to travel with strangers, but they were really presentable and well spoken.

They walked along and chatted, finding common ground. Their car was parked across the road, opposite one of the many entrances to the park. It was a green VW Beetle.

"There you go, Beatle girl. A car to match your name," joshed Ben.

"Not the right spelling but what's an 'e' or an 'a' between friends?" she quipped.

"Actually, it's mine," said Dave. "It's perfect for travelling over the Snake Pass to Sheffield."

Becca and Lynne sat in the back as the conversation continued all the way to town.

"I like Dave," whispered Lynne into Becca's ear.

"I like Ben. He's got my sense of humour, plus he's tall, dark and handsome, to coin a phrase," she murmured.

"So's Dave."

They arrived in the town centre and parked. As they walked to the café, Ben put his arm around Becca, and Dave followed suit with Lynne. The place was crowded, but they grabbed the table near the window when a group of people left.

"Would you like anything with your frothy coffees?" asked Ben.

"Cups would be a good idea," joshed Becca.

"What about saucers?" he replied sardonically.

"Those too."

"Cheeky."

Becca studied him as he queued at the counter. *He's a cross between Beatle Paul and John Alderton. Arched eyebrows and thick, dark hair. Plus, he's super intelligent with a great sense of fun. I'm impressed.*

As Lynne chatted to Dave, he kept looking across at Becca. He smiled at her, and she felt a bit uncomfortable because he was Lynne's date, so to speak. Becca got up and joined Ben in the queue to help him carry the coffees back to the table.

"What do we owe you for the drinks?" asked Becca.

"My treat," replied Ben.

"You sure?"

"Positive."

"Why, thank you, kind sir," she said with a salute, and Ben returned the salutation.

"So, what do you want to be when you finally grow up, Beatle girl," he asked with a wide smile.

"Happy. I want to be happy," she said with a frown, ignoring his sarcasm.

Ben saw a fleeting shadow across Becca's expressive face. *There's more to this joker than meets the eye.*

"We were in London last weekend. At Wembley no less, watching England win the world cup!" he informed them, changing the subject.

"Oh, fab!" exclaimed Becca. "Saturday 30th July 1966 will go down in football history. My dad told me there were over 96,000 people in the stadium. Not to mention the 32 million viewers following it on telly. It must be the UK's most watched event ever!"

"The extra time was so nerve-racking, but we did it. When they lifted up that trophy, it was the proudest moment," added Dave.

"I'm not into football, but I have to say it was something very special to see," agreed Lynne.

"I love football and go to see Manchester City play at Maine Road with my dad and brother, although I haven't been to as many matches recently."

"I'm a Manchester United supporter and I go to Old Trafford with high expectations," mocked Ben.

"I also go to Old Trafford, but only to watch George Best. Hats off to him for destroying Benefica 5-1, last March in Lisbon. They nicknamed him El Beatle. And that's music to my ears."

"So, The Beatles are your favourite group I take it?"

"Correct. Especially John and Paul. I have no words. They're simply magical."

"I prefer The Stones. Mind you, Lennon is a tour de force," acknowledged Ben.

"I think their latest LP 'Revolver' is brilliant. I could listen to it all day," commented Dave.

"So could I," said Lynne, feeling a bit out of it, especially as Dave kept looking more at Becca than herself.

The banter continued and eventually it was time to go home. They dropped Becca and Lynne off at their respective houses and made arrangements to see them again the following weekend. Becca was not too sure about Ben's character. She had observed him closely in the café and there was a mendacious expression in his eyes when he told her about his university life. She could not put her finger on it, but her intuition told her that he was not all he appeared to be.

He had written to her in the week. It was a very witty and entertaining letter. He was really looking forward to seeing her again at the weekend. Her physical attraction to him was strong and she felt it was mutual.

Once again, Dave drove Ben to Manchester and called for Becca and Lynne. They went to a charming, quaint restaurant in Alderley Edge and had lunch. Ben offered Becca a cigarette. She took one puff and choked.

"Bloody hell, that's really strong," she coughed.

"Player's No.6 fags are deadly. Try this one. It's menthol and cool," suggested Dave with a smile.

Becca actually liked it, but it was the worst thing she could have possibly enjoyed. After that she turned into a recurrent smoker, always the menthol cigarettes, but nevertheless it became a habit.

When they left, Ben grabbed Becca's hand and pulled her in a different direction to their friends. Becca leant against a secluded tree trunk, and he kissed her passionately. She could feel his arousal and his heart was beating fast. He slid his hand inside her blouse and felt her warm, soft breast. He unzipped his fly and exposed himself.

"You turn me on, Beatle girl," he said in a thick voice. "Fancy a fuck?"

Those last three words were the biggest turn-off she had ever heard. Not just the crass remark, but the glib way he suggested any intimacy. She pulled away from him, straightened her top and walked back to wait for Lynne and Dave in the car park.

He's a good-looking version of 'uncle' Ted.

"Aw, come on Becca, you know the score," he scowled. "Don't be a prick teaser."

"Why don't you just clear off back to your trough?"

"Oh well, if that's the way it's going to be, let's call it a day."

"I agree."

"Where's your airhead of a friend gone to with Dave?" he drawled.

Becca gave him a dirty look and waited for Lynne to come back. Ben disappeared into the restaurant and Becca just sat on an outside bench. When they did return, she asked if she could go home without any explanation.

Dave drove them back in silence. Lynne was really puzzled. It seemed just her and Dave were doing all the talking. In the back seat, Becca and Ben both gazed out of their windows, seeing nothing in particular.

Later on that evening, Lynne phoned up Becca to find out what had happened.

"He came on to me. All hands and no trousers, if you get my drift. Sheffield is welcome to him."

*

The next weekend, on Sunday, Becca was playing 'Revolver' for about the umpteenth time and singing along with Paul on the track 'Got to Get You Into My Life'. Her mother had given up banging on the ceiling with the brush handle. The volume was full blast, so Becca did not hear the front doorbell ring. Shirley answered it to find a presentable, good-looking stranger on the step.

"Hello. My name's Dave Phillips. I'm a friend of Becca's. Is she in?" he asked politely.

"Oh, she hasn't mentioned you. Where did you meet her?"

"In Heaton Park. She was with her friend, Lynne."

" Oh, I see. She didn't say you were coming today."

"No. It's a surprise."

"Just a minute," said Shirley, leaving Dave stood on the doorstep.

She waited until the record had stopped and shouted up the stairs.

"Becca! You've got a visitor. You better come down."

"Who is it?"

"A young man called Dave Phillips."

"Who?"

"Just come down, please."

Becca tutted. She was totally in her Beatle-zone and getting ready to belt out the next track. She checked herself in the mirror and pelted down the stairs. Her mother was still in the hall with the door wide open. Becca was rather surprised to see Dave. She was not that pleased either.

"Dave tells me you met him in the park with Lynne," explained Shirley, in an accusatory tone.

"I did. I mean we did. What do you want?" she puzzled.

"Can we talk? It won't take long," he requested.

"If it's about Ben, I'm not interested," she replied sharply.

"Who's Ben?" interrupted Shirley.

"He's no-one."

"It's nothing to do with Ben," explained Dave. "It's all to do with me. I just want to ask you something. It's important."

Becca saw a genuine expression in his appealing brown eyes and relented.

"OK. Let's talk in the garden," she agreed. "Mum, it's OK. We'll just pop round the back."

Shirley nodded but she was full of curiosity. *What's she been up to now?*

They walked to the bottom of the well-tended lawn, past the hedge that separated it from the vegetable patches and down some steps that led into a miniature grassy plot. Dave was impressed with the whole layout and wondered who had designed it.

"I love your garden. I've not seen such a well-ordered display of flowers and veg like this before."

"My dad's got green fingers. The whole area was a huge cinder track when he bought the house. He's cultivated the land. He's amazing."

"Why are there four holes in the large lawn?"

"Oh, he made me a putting green and put tin cans in the holes to trap the ball. It works. We still play it for fun."

"That's so cool."

"Look, Dave, what do you want? Why aren't you with Lynne? I don't know if Ben told you what happened, but he came on to me and I pushed him away. He's a jerk."

"He didn't elaborate but I guessed."

"So why are you here?"

"Because Ben doesn't deserve you. Becca, I fancied you from the minute we all met. It's just that Ben got there first, so I ended up with Lynne. She's a nice girl but she's not really my type."

"I see."

Becca's heart fluttered at the expression in his eyes. If she was honest with herself, she always thought that Dave was kind and thoughtful. He was also very handsome. Even more so, he was into The Beatles. That was a massive plus in itself.

"So, where do we go from here?" he queried.

"I don't know. If I go out with you, Lynne will be hurt. She's a close friend and I don't want to upset her."

"But I don't want to see her. Even if you weren't on the scene, I'd still feel the same way."

"This is so difficult. I don't want her to think she's been dumped because of me."

"So, do you want to go out with me, Becca?"

"Yes."

"Right then, leave it to me to explain things to Lynne. I'll let you know what happens. You just go back upstairs and sing with the Fab Four. I told you before that the 'Revolver' LP is a revelation. Oh, by the way, you've got a great voice. Paul would be flattered. You sound good together."

Becca smiled widely. "I love singing. Especially Beatle songs. My brother Mikey plays guitar, and he's recently taught me some more chords. Bob Dylan is my favourite solo singer-songwriter. His words are just mind-blowing."

"You'll have to play for me sometime. There's a folk club near my house. You can always sing there. I think you'll love it. They've got pictures of Dylan on the wall. Some great posters of him."

They looked at each other and neither of them moved until Dave bent down and kissed Becca on the cheek. Her skin tingled where his lips had been.

"Leave it to me, Beatle girl. I'll make it right with Lynne. Promise."

"Be gentle with her. She's a very dear friend. I hate upsetting the people I care about."

"So do I."

"Then we've got a lot in common." *He's the exact opposite to Ben. I really like him.*

*

Becca had invited Dave to her sixteenth birthday party. It fell on a Thursday, so she had an early celebration the weekend before. They were dating and totally in tune with each other. Lynne was rather upset at first and did not speak to Becca for a while. Then she met a student called Gary. She fell head over heels for him and Dave was relegated to the bottom of the league. As a result, her and Becca, were now the best of friends again and could even laugh about it all.

"I felt so bad about Dave, you know. But I think Ben did us both a great favour," giggled Becca, feeling tipsy after her second glass of cider.

"He sure did. I would never have met Gary if I was still with Dave."

"And I'd never have gone out with Dave if I'd fallen for Ben."

The Beatles records were invading the room on Becca's new audio system. It was a birthday present from her parents and Becca was in seventh heaven, listening to them through the large speakers.

"I think my mum has resigned herself to my Beatle world. It's four years since I first heard them, so that's plenty of time to get used to the volume, let alone the songs."

"Their songs just get better and better," remarked Dave. "But I've got to tell you that their concert on the 29th August at Candlestick Park, in San Francisco, was their last one. Touring is killing them. Remember that trip to Asia in July? Well, it culminated in a scary incident in the Philippines. They'd unknowingly snubbed the nation's first family, and the people turned against them in a horrible way. Suddenly they were without police protection. They had to defend themselves against multiple irate nationalists who manhandled them every step of the way to the airport."

"What! I didn't realise it was that bad!" protested Becca.

"Oh, it got far worse in the US."

"Yes, I know. You mean the Ku Klux Klan and all those religious zealots who stirred it all up because of that off the cuff comment that John made about Jesus?"

"They got death threats and bullet holes on the fuselage of their plane! That proved the zealots meant dangerous business! They were heading into a perilous storm of protest. But let me tell you, Becca, that they are at death's door as musicians. The thrill of playing to a crowd is tarnished and the hysterical fame has robbed them of everything that made it wonderful," he explained.

"My poor boys. I know that the arenas are far too large, and the screams overpower the amplifiers so they can't even hear what they're singing. The music has nothing to do with it anymore. No wonder they're pulling the plug on these concerts. They just aren't enjoying any of it."

"Do you know that a firecracker exploded in Memphis when they were performing? They thought that a gunman had gone on a rampage and that the assassination threats were becoming an actuality. In Cincinnati, it rained at an open-air concert. They were scared of being electrocuted and wanted to cancel the show. But that would also cause a riot among the 35,000 fans, so it was a no-win situation. Everyone chanted "we want The Beatles" and Paul was so churned up about the whole thing that he threw up in the dressing room."

"Oh, my God, Dave. How do you know this in such detail?"

"I have a friend who's a journalist. He gets to know all the background information. He told me that their roadie, Mal Evans, got such an electric shock that day that he was thrown across the stage. The show was postponed until the day after.

"In fact, this happened again in St. Louis when it poured. Apparently, they put bits of corrugated iron over the stage, so it felt like the worst little gig they'd ever played at, even before they'd started as a band. They were worried about the rain getting in the amps and this took them right back to the Cavern days. It was worse than those early years in Hamburg. Seemingly there were sparks flying all over the place. It went from bad to worse as the tour continued. So many reasons why they want the live performances to be a thing of the past."

"Oh, my word. It's so sad. I was one of those screaming banshees! I mean, it wasn't in a huge stadium, but nevertheless I just couldn't stop. It must have been so frightening for them when it was on a massive scale What's the point of singing your heart out if the audience can't hear you? I've known for ages that John wasn't happy with all of this. But I didn't realise it was affecting the group as a whole."

"Can you imagine thousands of fans breaking through the barriers? The thought of it was terrifying."

"Oh heck. I tried to climb on stage at the ABC to get to John and Paul. I just went wild. In my case it was a knee-jerk reaction to a three-year wait to actually see them play. But even so, I regret it now. I can't explain the effect they have on me. My admiration is far more than ten rows back in a theatre, screaming my head off like a stupid child. They're in my blood. I feel like I've known them in a previous life. That sounds crazy but that's how it is for me. They saved me, Dave."

"From what?"

"I can't talk about it. All I know is that without their music, I would have had an even tougher time. I wouldn't have coped."

"Coped with what, Becca? You can tell me."

"I can't. It's vile and it's still going on. The only difference is that I can rise above it. But it's still left a deep scar."

'Uncle' Ted, you've a lot to answer for. A lifetime in jail would not be enough.

Chapter Eight

By the time 1967 had settled in comfortably, Becca had reached a determined conclusion. She would take her long-awaited O-Levels and leave without fuss or decoration in the heat of the lazy summer. She had decided to go to a technical college of sorts, which would probably result in a dead-end job, the other side of the moon.

I truly don't care. What the hell. I have to get out of this academic abyss. I don't know if I'm ready for the gaping jaws of the outside world just yet. But I have to escape.

She borrowed Mikey's acoustic guitar and improved her technique. She had added a few more chords to her usual ones and finger-plucking came into being, as well as strumming. It crystallised easily. Just like a marigold loves the sun. She was soon playing along to Beatle classics and was reborn. She had something more than a record collection. She could recreate the music herself. She was elated to perform those songs that had afforded her so much jubilation.

Dave took her to a variety of folk clubs, both local and in Sheffield. Her appreciation of Bob Dylan was instrumental in searching for songs with underplay and meaning. She discovered, with breathless realisation, that the stage was her home ground and music made the world go round. So that was why she was more than ready for 'Sgt. Pepper' and beautiful flowers in her hair.

John had taken a break away from the group and had been filming his solo acting part for the film *How I Won the War.* It took place last autumn in 1966, with the release date scheduled for the 18th October 1967. It was a surreal black comedy, and he played the part of Musketeer Gripweed. In preparation for the role, he had his hair cut short, contrasting discernibly with his Beatle image. He also wore round 'granny' glasses. As he was near-sighted, he then donned this particular style for the rest of his life. They became iconic and Becca just loved him more than ever.

During his time filming in Almería, John had rented a villa with his wife, Cynthia. His co-star was Michael Crawford, who was married to Gabrielle Lewis, and the foursome stayed there. The villa's wrought iron gates and surroundings reminded John of Strawberry Fields, the Salvation Army garden near his boyhood home.

On the 13th February 1967, The Beatles released their double A-side single 'Penny Lane' coupled with John's 'Strawberry Fields Forever', the song he was inspired to write while actually filming. Penny Lane is a road in the Liverpool suburb of Mossley Hill. Paul wrote it out of nostalgia because it was a place that he and John knew well. Apparently, Paul would get a bus to John's house, or John would do the same to his. They had to change at the roundabout terminus. Their co-written lyrics of the song vividly reflected those memories.

Becca knew Penny Lane very well because her Uncle David and Aunty Rose lived close by, and the single brought back many recollections of her own childhood. She recognised all the places and people they were singing about. She felt that she belonged in the song.

On the 26th May 1967 their eighth studio LP, 'Sgt. Pepper's Lonely Hearts Club Band', was released. As ever, Becca's dad, Eric, had purchased it for her. She was very excited because they had not recorded a new LP since 'Revolver' last year. It was their first studio double album and Becca was breathless with anticipation when she placed vinyl disc number one on the turntable. The front cover alone was incredible, and her hands were trembling as she waited for the first song to play.

She did not have to keep stopping and starting it in order to write down the lyrics because they were printed inside the sleeve. She sat on the bed and was totally blown away. It was a ground-breaking shift in music, and a kick in the teeth to those who thought The Beatles were over when they stopped touring. Becca's eyes were as kaleidoscopic as 'Lucy in the Sky', with or without the diamonds. She spent hours listening to albums one and two, totally entranced and transported. Her imagination was on fire by proxy.

Bye-bye mopheads and hello to pushing boundaries! The cover alone is an art form! And the songs! The arrangements! The orchestral sounds! I'm speechless. A very unusual state for me. My O-Levels will definitely fly out the window now. I'm due to take them soon. The only memorising I'll be doing is a thorough revision of Sgt. Pepper!

Oh, God! Nearly five years on and I'm more hooked than ever before. I always thought they were magical. Was I right or what? This is solid proof. How can anyone criticise them after this masterpiece of creative engineering by George Martin. It's pure genius. I love The Beatles with all my heart and boots. Even their moustaches.

Just look at their outfits! Long silk coats and trousers to match. John in lime, Paul in blue, George in tangerine and Ringo in deep pink. The Fab Four with officers' fringed epaulettes, intermingled with a variety of other insignia. It's surreal. It's not just off the wall, it's totally up my street and in the middle of the bloody road! I love it, love it, love it.

John's lost weight. His eyes look dead. Eh? I must be imagining this. He's not plagued anymore by screaming fans storming the stage. I think he's taken something. They probably all have. Some of the lyrics sound drug induced.

What am I going to do about my life? I can't live it as a Beatle extension. I need my own identity. I'll have to take it day by day. If I think too far ahead, it makes my head spin. I don't know where I belong. Never have really. Maybe when I was very little, surrounded by unconditional love. That was easier. But now, I feel I'm on the brink of something indefinite. It's almost as if I can reach out and grab it but I'm not sure of what I'm snatching. Music is definitely a huge part of it. So is poetry. So is art.

On the 7th July, The Beatles released their fifteenth single, 'All You Need Is Love', with the flip side 'Baby You're a Rich Man'. Becca, by this time, looked like a flower child with attitude. A suburban hippy that stood out like a sore thumb. But that was the intention anyway.

'All You Need is Love' was written specifically for *Our World,* which was a televised satellite link-up between twenty-five worldwide countries on the 25th June 1967. It was the first of its kind and it captured the idealistic mood of 'the summer of love'.

Becca was with Dave, watching it at his house along with several friends. Not all of them made allowances for her jack-in-the-box antics. She lit up another cigarette to calm herself down.

"Dave! Just look at the Fabs! What a brilliant song, with an even greater message. It's John's baby. He's chewing gum and looks so cool, even with the headphones on. So many celebrities in the audience with them. There's Jagger! He's enraptured by the looks of it. My beautiful Beatles. Now they really are reaching out to the world, just like I saw when I was thirteen years old. I prophesied this and the feeling was so intense. It's like I had a hotline to their destiny."

"Cool it," said a student. "It's all about being laid back."

"This is me. Take it or leave it. It's nothing to do with you. It's all to do with them," she replied, blowing out a stream of smoke right into his face.

"Becca's obsessed with The Beatles. They can do no wrong in her eyes. So let her celebrate this special programme. It's allowed," defended Dave.

"Whatever floats her boat. I prefer The Who."

"Fine. I prefer to dance on the ceiling when I look and listen to John and Paul."

"What about George and Ringo? It's not just a duo, you know."

"Thanks for telling me. I'll make a note in my diary that on this day, I discovered there were actually four Beatles. Silly me. I was never any good at maths."

"So, what are you taking?"

"Taking?"

"Yeah. At university. What are you reading?"

"I'm still at school and in the middle of my O-Levels. 'O' for opinionated. A bit like you!"

"How old are you, Miss Clever Clogs?"

"Seventeen in September. Why?"

"Cheeky little bugger, aren't you?"

"I really appreciate you taking the time to express that," she mocked, and Dave laughed out loud.

*

As the last papers of the O-Level examinations were collected by a stripe-tied android, Becca left the hall for the final time. She walked through the lingering strictness of the corridors, remembering the events of the last five years.

She recalled a twelve-year-old apparition with white socks and a shiny face, polished satchel and navy gymslip. She recollected, with great clarity, the contagious impact of the early Beatles years. The Lennon lovers. The McCartney addicts. The Harrison brigade. The Starr procession. She remembered the pranks and endless hanky-panky. She remembered the wild buzz of popularity and the murky blues of the detention room. She remembered the Christmas end of term concerts. She remembered the Beatle Monthly magazines that were forever being confiscated. She remembered the whispered secrets and confessions of thirteen-year-old playmates.

For a long time now, she had wanted to escape the trappings of her educational masquerade, and now it was here, all she could think of was the closeness she had attained with her long-term friends. She was not just leaving behind a deep frustration. She was breaking away from a crowd of people she had learnt to love. If that large building could have related all that had occurred within its walls, what a story it would tell to future scholars. As it stood, those memories would be lost forever, and wiped away by another generation with their own ideas and dreams.

She broke down in an alcove with her closest friends. Where would they all go? What would they all do? Would it all be worth it? Was it really five years since the first flicker of friendship? They promised to write, but in her heart she knew that future passions would triumph and new friends could replace old ones.

But before she left completely, there was one last mark of protest she needed to perform. She had brought with her The Beatles single which was riding high in the charts, and took it out of her briefcase. She made her way into the assembly hall, high on adrenaline and rebellion. At the back of the stage there was a sound system which was used for playing classical music as part of the lessons. It was also utilised for concerts or speeches. She found the turntable and placed the single 'All You Need Is Love' on the top. Then she switched it on, full blast. As it reverberated around the whole school, pupils came running in to see what was happening.

Becca was stood on the stage, bold as brass in absolute defiance. The Headmistress's study was close by, and she stormed into the hall with an expression of pure horror.

"Rebecca Beacon! I might have known! You're outrageous! Switch that dreadful music off, right now! You're expelled!"

"It's nearly finished, and I'm leaving today anyway. Sorry you won't have the satisfaction of getting rid of me. Let's hear it for freedom of expression, Mrs. Shaw! After all, listen to the words. All you need is love! It's magical. Goodbye detentions. Farewell to the strap. As for me? Watch this bloody space! Oh, and long live The Beatles!"

*

The flower power reign was ruling supreme. A new cult of people, originating in San Francisco, were tickling the insides of major cities. The shanty town hippies were setting up communes in many places. The day-to-day workers from stuffy offices could throw off their shackles and taste a new kind of freedom, if they wished to embrace the trend. Young men were wearing coloured beads, kaftans and Indian headbands around their shoulder-length tresses. Girls were in fringed jackets and long, printed dresses, with flowers in their hair.

Becca was marvelling at the whole movement as she witnessed the changing creativity within the music world. She realised completely why the obliteration of those strength-sapping and mind-draining tours was so vital for her icons. All energies were being ploughed into new sounds with a freshness of delivery. Sounds capturing willow-tree sadness, oriental observances, synthesised consistency, psychedelic fantasy, rainbow niceties and glowing awareness. The Sgt. Pepper compositions were almost conceptual. Each song was different and possessed a distinctive sound. And yet it all came together as a whole.

On the 25th August, The Beatles journeyed to Bangor, Wales, by train. They were attending a seminar on transcendental meditation, held by the Indian teacher Maharishi Mahesh Yogi. The interest was sparked by drug-induced experiences after John and George used them in an effort to expand their consciousness. As a result, their minds were wide open to achieving inner peace and awareness.

It was the first time for several years that they had travelled without their manager Brian Epstein, or their tour managers. They had not even thought to bring any cash with them. They arrived at London's Euston Station late in the afternoon and were enmeshed in a large crowd, made unfavourable by the fact that it was the Friday before the UK's late summer Bank Holiday weekend. They were left to carry their own cases and were besieged on their way to the platform. John's wife, Cynthia, became segregated from the group. Mistaken for a fan, she was detained by police officers. Peter Brown from NEMS arranged for Neil Aspinall to drive her to Bangor by road. It was a stressful and unsettling experience.

On the 26th August they had a press conference and declared that they were going to give up hallucinogenic drugs, which was in accordance with the Maharishi's teachings. He also advised them to steer clear of the 'Ban the Bomb' movement and to support the appointed government of the day. The intention was to take part in the whole of the ten-day seminar, but their stay was cut short by the tragic death of their manager Brian Epstein on the 27th August.

Ironically, Becca was in the front room of her friend's house, playing guitar and singing a Beatles song, when the news came through. Jane's mother told them it had just been announced on the radio. Becca had been prepared for many changes that summer, but she was nowhere near ready for the shock of his demise. For a moment, the room was filled with a stunned silence. She looked at Jane who stared speechlessly back at her, totally dumbfounded at the unreal report that he had died of an overdose of barbiturates.

"How? When? Why?" questioned Becca when she found her voice.

"Poor Eppy. Oh, my word. He was only thirty-two," gasped Jane.

Although the main attraction had always been the group, there was not one Beatles fan who failed to realise the huge part that Brian had played in their promotion and success. He was also the backbone of a string of artists, that were part of the whole Liverpool scene.

He had hand-picked The Beatles from out of their Hamburg apprenticeship and ambitious obscurity. He scratched, battled and pressed with the cut-throat world of recording untouchables to recognise an exciting potential. He was the epitome of organisation and charm. He had it all and now, suddenly, he was wiped off the face of the earth as rapidly as the speed of sound.

She went back mentally in time to The Cavern Club. Even though she was too young to have been a part of that scenario, she had read all about those early days. She knew that Brian first noticed The Beatles in issues of *Mersey Beat* and on numerous posters around Liverpool. The editor of the magazine, Bill Harry, had featured her icons on the front page of its second issue. The Beatles had recorded 'My Bonnie' as a single with Tony Sheridan while they were in Germany.

Brian's interpretation of the story was that a customer, Raymond Jones, came into the record department of his family's newly opened NEMS music store on Great Charlotte Street in Liverpool and asked for 'My Bonnie' by The Beatles. Brian had laboured day and night at the store to make it a success and it became one of the largest musical retail outlets in northern England. Through his industrious work, he acquired substantial knowledge of the pop music business.

The Beatles were due to perform a lunchtime concert at The Cavern Club on the 9th November 1961. Brian and his assistant, Alistair Taylor, were permitted to enter without queuing. Bob Wooler, the resident DJ, disclosed a welcoming message over the club's public address system, telling everyone that they had a famous visitor in the audience. What ensued after Brian was introduced to The Beatles backstage was the beginning of a phenomenal success story that would shake up the world.

Back in the present, Becca held her friend's guitar very close to her body. It was as if she was clinging on to the past and it symbolised the end of an era. *I've got a feeling that things will get very complicated. I think Eppy felt surplus to requirements when 'his boys' stopped touring. After all, he was the one that organised all their appearances. He adored them. And now he's no longer here. So, who will take his place?*

"Do you want a cup of tea and some sponge cake, Becca?" asked Jane's mother in a caring manner.

Becca was staring into space. Her thoughts were very active.

This is so weird. Jane and I were singing 'You've Got to Hide Your Love Away' when we were told the news. I know that Brian was homosexual, but in my books any kind of loving is fine. Maybe he couldn't really come to terms with it. It's only a month ago on the 27th July that it was decriminalised. About bloody time!

This is so moving because he could have lived his life openly and embraced his sexuality. So very unjust and sad. I'm a Libran and all for justice. It's come rather too late for Brian. RIP, you special man.

"Becca, are you all right?"

"What?"

"Are you OK? You look so upset."

"I am."

"I understand. It's a horrible ending at such a young age," commented Jane's mother. "Do you think he took an overdose on purpose?"

"I don't think so. He loved his mother too much to do that. Maybe he just wanted to blot stuff out and it went wrong. I don't know. It's tragic."

"Yes, it is. Anyway, I asked you if you would like some tea with a piece of cake. I only baked it this morning."

"A cup of tea would be nice, with two sugars please. Not so sure if I can eat the cake at the minute. My stomachs in knots."

"And mine," remarked Jane with sad eyes.

Becca was unconsciously pressing so hard on the fretboard of the guitar that the steel strings nearly cut through her fingertips.

"It will affect their future. I know it will. They'll be like a ship without a rudder."

"Surely not. They'll find someone to manage them. There'll be a stampede of impresarios wanting to sign The Beatles. I don't think it will be a problem," commented Jane.

"It will rock the boat. Especially now that they're a studio band only. God only knows which way they'll go. It could be the beginning of the end. I pray that I'm entirely wrong."

For days after the tragic event, Becca felt a heaviness usually reserved for the emptiness and sadness after the death of someone close to the heart. It was almost as if she had psychically sensed the future acrimony and chaos that his departure undoubtedly effected.

*

When Becca received the news that she had passed five O-Levels she nearly fainted, because the only form of revision undertaken that summer had been a thorough research of 'Sgt. Pepper's Lonely Hearts Club Band'.

"See! See what you could have done if you'd really concentrated on your exams! You should have stayed on and taken your A-Levels!" berated her mother.

"Mum, I couldn't have spent one more hour in that domineering den, with that hard-nosed headmistress and her stroppy staff."

"So what are you going to do?"

"I've already decided. I'm going to do typing, shorthand, and liberal studies at technical college. It's just a fill-in because the main aim is to sing and write. But I can get a job with those skills and be independent."

"You'll have to get good results otherwise you'll be back to square one."

"Oh, I'll be fine. I'll make sure that I do well. It's all part of the plan."

"Plan?"

"Yes. Everything is fated. I didn't clap eyes on The Beatles for fun. They'll always be around even when they've disbanded. I play folk songs at various university circuits. Dave takes me and I get a good reaction. The only thing is, I have to borrow Dave's guitar. I really could do with one of my own. When I'm working, I can pay for everything I need towards a career in music. Because that's the main aim, Mum."

"It's a pipe dream, Becca."

"No, it isn't. I can sing and play guitar. I've not written an original song yet, but it will happen. In the meantime, I love singing songs with meaning. Those melodies with poetical lyrics set to music. They're wonderful."

"How are you going to write music when you can't read it?"

"How did The Beatles write all their songs? They can't read a note."

"Ah, so we're back to the mopheads again. Five years on and you're still bewitched."

"Not in the same way as when I was twelve years old. I love them dearly, but I respect their creativity without having to yell or scream when I see them. My heart still flutters with passion, but in a more mature sense. There's no denying that I'm still attracted to John and Paul physically, but they've stirred up a longing to immerse myself in a creative career. I can't get that from academia."

"But you'll have to adhere to certain rules at college. You're still under their control."

"Not really. Lynne's sister is at college, and she says that they treat her like an adult, even when she rails against something. It's called free speech. Without a detention in the offing."

Shirley could see that Becca was determined to carve out her own path. Once her mind was set on something, it would never deviate from that purpose.

"Well, I guess this is the way forward for you. But let me tell you something from my own experience. The music world is highly competitive and full of sharks. You'll need to be strong-minded, otherwise you're in for a bumpy ride. I think working towards a proper job is the right way forward. You can always sing as a hobby."

"Mum, I want to sing and write, full stop. The only reason I'm going to college is to obviously gain certain skills and make money to buy a guitar, keyboard or piano. I also need different clothes for the stage, so that will come out of my wages. Anyway, it's a two-year course, so there's plenty of time to perfect my act. When I played at the Rag Ball in Sheffield, thanks to Dave, it went down really well. More than I thought it would. I was on fire and the audience knew it."

"Right then, well, before you burst into flames, please take these eggs round to your aunty Doreen," said Shirley, changing the subject completely.

The son of a local farmer delivered eggs once a week. Shirley always bought an extra dozen for her sister because she was forever baking and cooking. She did not want to be reimbursed but Doreen always insisted on doing so.

"Aw, Mum. I'm in the middle of listening to Sgt. Pepper."

"I've lost count of how many times you've played it! It's a wonder that the vinyl has still got grooves! For heaven's sake, just give it a rest. Anyway, your aunty Doris was saying that she hasn't seen you for ages. Not to mention your grandfather, who loves you to bits."

"I know. I've been too busy with this and that."

"Well, go and see all of them and fill them in with 'this and that'. They'll be interested in your plans."

"Aunty Doris and Gramps will. Not Aunty Doreen! She thinks I'm as mad as a box of frogs."

"She might have a point."

Becca double-crossed her eyes and pulled a face. Shirley tried to stifle her amusement, but the expression was so comical that she laughed out loud.

"Becca Beacon, you're one on your own. A complete enigma. But I love you with all my heart."

"And boots," added Becca.

"Boots?"

"That's my catchphrase now. I love you with all my heart and boots."

"Talking of boots, yours need heeling."

"Will you take them to the cobblers for me, please? I'm too busy organising stuff and Dave's throwing an all-night party this weekend."

"Is he indeed? And where will my rebellious daughter be staying all night?"

"At Jane's. Or maybe at Lynne's. I'll probably leave around midnight and be sleeping over with one of them, at either house."

"Hmm."

"Truly."

"Just promise me one thing, Becca. No drugs! It's bad enough that you smoke."

"Mum, I don't need drugs. My imagination is my fix."

"Well still be careful. Watch out for your drink being spiked."

"I swear I'll keep a vigil over my glass at all times."

"Stay close to Dave. He's a very nice young man. Thoughtful and kind."

"I agree. So don't worry."

*

The party was in full swing, and the music was booming. Becca was in her hippy-trippy element. She wore a long denim skirt with tiny bells sewn into the side seams that jangled when she moved. Her top was a chiffon, flower-patterned creation with flared sleeves. She had grown her hair and had a floral headband around her forehead to match her blouse. Open-toed navy sandals completed the picture, accompanied by a solid silver ankle bracelet with a tiny charm in the shape of a heart. Multiple silver bracelets adorned both wrists.

There was a huge crowd of people, mostly Dave's friends from university, and some strangers who had gatecrashed the gathering. Marijuana joints were being passed around like sweets and joss sticks filled the room with a strong smell of incense. The Beatles records were centre stage. John and Paul were singing 'A Day in The Life' and Becca joined them with her own rendition.

"Hey, you've got a groovy voice," said a student called Phil, and Becca thanked him for the compliment.

"She's going to entertain us soon, aren't you?" encouraged Dave.

"For sure. Where's your guitar, Dave? It always needs tuning."

"In the other room. Do you want it now?"

"Soon. I just want to hear some more Beatles tracks."

"For the millionth time, huh?" Dave smiled.

"More like the billionth," she confirmed.

"Do you dig The Beatles?" asked Phil.

"No. It's just a rumour," she quipped.

"Do you know them personally?"

"Oh, I know them all right. I was introduced in 1962. Five years later and we're still going strong."

"Hey, that's so cool. What's your name?"

"Beatle girl."

Their conversation was interrupted by an impromptu visit from the law. The neighbours had reported the incessant noise, and one of them had seen some students in the back garden smoking pot. Becca's friend, Jane, ran over to her and panicked.

"Becca, it's the police. They'll arrest us for possessing cannabis."

"I haven't touched it but you're right. Let's go hide."

Dave was trying his best to remove all traces of the

drug as Becca and Jane ran upstairs. They climbed out of a bedroom window onto the roof over the kitchen extension.

"Lie down flat and don't say a word," instructed Becca.

It began to pour, and the absurdity of their situation set them off into a fit of restrained giggles.

"It's you, Becca," Jane whispered. "Everywhere we go. First the fog, now the rain. I'm soaked."

"Shh. There's a copper on the lawn and he's looking our way. He's seen us!"

"All right, girls! I'm coming up to talk to you. This is a drugs raid and you're obviously avoiding me," he said sardonically.

"Oh, no, Officer. We were just stargazing and then it rained," fibbed Becca.

"And lying down on a wet roof is perfect for looking into space. Pull the other one, it's got bells on," he ridiculed.

"That would be my skirt. It's got bells all down both sides. See?" joked Becca, standing up to jiggle and jingle.

"OK, little miss wisecracker. I'm on my way up, so make your way back into the house."

They both tried not to laugh. Then Becca appeared momentarily concerned.

"See! I now get into trouble out of school, even when it's not my fault. I hope this isn't a detention of the unlawful kind. I'm innocent your honour!"

Dave and friends had done a lightning job of getting rid of any wacky-backy evidence. The smell of pot still lingered in the rooms, but the aroma of the joss sticks was just as pungent. They were just cautioned to tone down the noise and have consideration for their neighbours.

Upstairs, Becca and Jane were being questioned by the young officer. They both looked drenched from the unexpected shower beforehand. He could find absolutely no trace of any illegal drugs, either on them or in the room. They breathed a sigh of relief when he left.

"Phew! That was close, even though we'd done nothing wrong. The irony is that I wouldn't touch drugs with a bargepole," affirmed Becca.

When she had dried off and made herself look appealing, she searched for Dave's guitar. It was against the wall in his bedroom. One of her favourite songs of the year was playing downstairs. Procul Harum were singing 'A Whiter Shade of Pale'. She loved Gary Brooker's voice. It was so soulful, and the music typified the whole essence of 1967 and the summer of love.

Becca eventually sat on a stool in the main room with the guitar and sang to her attentive audience. It was a mixture of folk and contemporary songs. Her voice was pure and strong, and she revelled in the moment. The applause was a different kind of music to her ears. She felt euphoric.

"Becca, sing a Beatles song," requested Dave.

She nodded and strummed her way through her last number, 'I'll Follow the Sun', and finished on a high as everyone cheered.

Oh yes. I'll follow the sun all right. Thank you, John and Paul, for showing me the way to go. I hope I did justice to your song. I feel so blessed that I was born into your era. I love you both. Forever.

*

Becca began her first term at college in September 1967. Unlike school, the atmosphere was more casual with an adult feel to the lectures. The difference was dramatic, and after the first month she found herself at the centre of a new social structure. Students were trusted to get on with their studies and were rarely reprimanded. However, the ultimate setback to this freedom was potential expulsion at the end of the year if carefree attitudes overpowered the lectures or learning.

Everyone expected to be treated as adults, and in return the teachers desired full time co-operation. As a result, she picked up shorthand very quickly and could also touch-type effortlessly. Her lecturer was very pleased with her progress so early in the term, and Becca gave herself a mental pat on the back for diligence. She loved the liberal studies because she wrote speeches about peace, love, understanding and justice, all those subjects close to her heart.

Her life became a whirlpool of activity and she found new friends, particularly two girls called Jean and Julie. After five years of being categorised and restrained, she wanted to enjoy every bit of liberality that the college offered, including the friendship of its many students. She became quite close with Aarkesh, who was a Hindu, and his friend Kamaari. She was fascinated by their culture and embraced them both willingly. They believed that each person was divine, and that the purpose of life was to seek and realise the divinity in all of us.

There was one particular student called Gregory who was bullied mercilessly for looking unkempt and gawky.

Becca could not join in with the browbeating because she thought it was cruel and mean. He had a hard home life, and it affected his whole personality. So, she made it her business to seek him out at lunchtimes and engage in some conversation.

Some of my new circle are out of order. Gregory is a sensitive soul and should be treated with kindness and compassion. I'm not a joiner-inner at the best of times, and in this particular case I won't be one of the heartless in-crowd.

"Why do you talk to that nerd?" asked Jean. "He's such a wimp."

"He's human. He's also intelligent and I don't judge a book by its cover."

"I can't stand to be near him. He reeks. I don't know when he last washed."

"I'm not with him long enough. A few kind words here and there are all he wants."

"You're something else, Becca. One minute the radical, the next Mother Theresa. Still, whatever floats your boat, Beatle girl."

"There's a common denominator with Gregory. He loves The Beatles. So, we chat about the music more than anything."

"Talking of the Fabs, have you heard their latest single?"

"You mean 'Hello, Goodbye'? Yeah, my dad bought it for me. It's good but I prefer the flip side, 'I Am the Walrus'. I love the Salvador Dali approach to words. It's brilliant."

"It's a bit daft though. It doesn't make any sense," commented Jean.

"It doesn't have to. It's called poetic licence and so typical of John's lyrics. I think it's a masterpiece of surrealism set to music."

"Whatever that means. Anyway, we're putting on a concert at the end of term. Are you going to play for us?"

"I'll have to borrow my boyfriend's guitar. He won't mind. So, yes, count me in."

*

Becca's workload began to suffer. She was so engrossed in the exhilarating taste of sociability that her studies went by the board. To top it all, she knew deep down that the course she was taking was only an escape from grammar school life, so she began to adopt the attitude of an all-time student. Whenever the subject of the outside world was mentioned, she shut her eyes and ears to it, refusing to contemplate the end result of all her studies.

The Beatles released the EP 'Magical Mystery Tour' on the 8th December 1967. A film had been in the making of the same name and would be televised on Boxing Day in black and white, to round off their musical year. It had been originally shot beforehand between the 11th and the 25th September. A colour transmission was to be shown the following year on the 5th January 1968. It was badly received by pundits and viewers, although the accompanying soundtrack was a profit-making and praiseworthy success. It gave birth to even more imaginative songs, such as 'Blue Jay Way' and 'The Fool on the Hill'.

Much of it was shot in and around RAF West Malling, a deactivated military airfield in Kent. The script was largely off the cuff. It went ahead on the foundation of a handwritten compilation of ideas. The film was intermingled with musical intervals. The situation was that of a group of people in a coach and involved several peculiar activities in surreal surroundings.

Becca's Christmas holidays were enlivened by her icons' self-produced fantasy film. The 'Magical Mystery Tour' added even more magic and mystery to her eternal reverence, regardless of its critical reception. The more it was derided by the critics and the public, the more Becca stood by her icons with unstinting allegiance.

On New Year's Eve 1967, she realised that she had 'known' The Beatles for over half a decade. In all that time her loyalty had never waned. If anything, she felt more for them than ever before. She could never get enough of their ever-changing creativity. Everything they produced, whether planned, experimental or impulsive, fed her vivid imagination and resulted in exultation.

A host of one-time fans preferred them as they were in the past and could not keep up with their musical or visual changes. A new generation were growing up into an altered era of Beatles influence, not remembering with the same vivid clarity as herself the mop haired image of 1963. She contemplated once again on Brian Epstein's premature death.

I wonder how much it will affect their bonded harmony and brotherhood? Four incredible musicians and songwriters, living constantly in each other's pockets, without firm management, could very likely result in a breakdown of sorts.

Regardless of all her negative thoughts, even she did not fully realise the exactness of her contemplation. All she felt was a creeping awareness of something disconcerting on the horizon. She wrote another short poem to try and capture her uncertainty.

When candyfloss is in your hand
And summertime is in command
Ten silver suns attract your eye
As fleeting sleeping skylines die
When daytime pleasure falls to waste
And nighttime calls in darkened haste
Black stars are climbing in my mind
My inky thoughts will soon unwind
So, who are you to ask me why
The clouds are shifting in the sky?

Regardless of her lackadaisical attitude and reluctance to embrace an inevitable nine-to-five existence, she did exceptionally well in her end of term examinations. The lecturer told her that it was tantamount to a distinction for her typing and shorthand skills. Her parents were very pleased with her apparent diligence. Becca just marvelled at the fact that very little effort was needed to obtain such a good result. She patted herself on the back and went along with the subterfuge.

Her mind went back to the summer when she had travelled to Bispham, in Blackpool, to stay with her aunty Mary and cousin Lisa. They had moved away to begin a new life after her aunty had divorced her perverse husband, Don. She had bought a bungalow from the proceeds of the house and quite a large sum of alimony was awarded to her in order to manage her financial affairs. They had both struggled with mental health issues, but their new surroundings helped them heal. There was no association with their turbulent past. The family visited them often and it was appreciated.

Becca and Lisa went to see Jimmy Tarbuck at the ABC in Blackpool because he made them howl with laughter and he looked like a fifth Beatle. Becca had actually joined his fan club and had several of her poems printed in the monthly magazines. She became very friendly with the secretary, Pattie Shine, and they corresponded regularly.

Laughter is definitely the best medicine. Just look at Lisa! She's much happier now. And Jimmy is so funny. But I've still got a creeping premonition that next year will be turbulent. And it's all to do with my beloved Beatles. Let's see what 1968 brings. And if I'm prepared for the changes.

Chapter Nine

In mid-February 1968, The Beatles travelled to Rishikesh, India, to take part in a Transcendental Meditation Course with the Maharishi Mahesh Yogi. It was John and George who specifically believed firmly in its worthiness. They became spokesmen for the movement and the Maharishi gained worldwide standing as guru to The Beatles. This experience, away from the hustle and bustle of the world at large, gave birth to the most high-yielding chapter for song writing, both collectively and individually. Eighteen of those melodies would be recorded for the next album. Others were used for future projects.

Becca was fascinated by their trip, especially the whole premise of meditation. She discussed it with her Hindu friends, who enlightened her on the benefits of engaging in mental exercise for the purpose of reaching a heightened level of spiritual awareness. Her brain was always racing at a million miles an hour, so learning these techniques would help her relax.

Apple Corps Ltd. was originally conceived by The Beatles in 1967 after Brian Epstein's death, to carry on with his plans. It was meant to be a small group of companies, in order to create a tax-effective business structure. Primarily, it would be an umbrella for all their creative endeavours. Their seventeenth single 'Lady Madonna', coupled with 'The Inner Light', was released on the 15th March 1968 on their newly formed Apple label.

Around this time, Becca was starting to get nasal problems that caused endless sinus infections and breathing difficulties. When she was a child, she had been hit on the bridge of her nose with a cricket ball and it had damaged the bone. As a result, she had a bump in the middle, which was evident in profile. In her mind it was huge, but according to her family and friends, not forgetting her boyfriend Dave, they thought it added character to her face. *I hate it. I want a nose with a normal bridge. I'm going to see about it. Aunty Doris said she'd come with me because my mum thinks I'm going over the top again.*

Shirley was baking some cakes when Becca announced her nose project.

"Are you doing this for vanity or medical reasons?" queried her mother.

"Both. I can't breathe properly, and I look like Ringo."

"Don't be ridiculous, Becca! You look absolutely nothing like him. It's all in your mind."

"No, it's all in my nose. It needs to be reshaped. Anyway, I've got an appointment with a surgeon next week and Aunty Doris is coming with me."

"Is she now? She never told me."

"That's because I told her not to."

"Why?"

"Because I know you'd try and put me off. It's quite a big operation I believe. It comes under plastic surgery."

"There's a massive waiting list for this kind of thing."

"I know. But when I see the nose man, I'll get round him and try and bring the date forward."

"That I can believe! You'd get round the big bad wolf if you had to! I don't put anything past my darling, daredevil daughter. You're a total one-off."

"You've told me that at least a thousand times."

"Because it's true! Anyway, what about your studies? Will it interfere with your lectures?"

"I don't know. That's why I've got this appointment. I need to weigh it all up."

"Hmm."

*

Unbeknown to her mother, Becca had already applied for a transfer to another smaller college nearer home which was more accessible. If accepted, she would start a new term before the summer. Her studies were becoming more and more neglected because her social life was intense. She did not want her frivolities to interfere with exam results. She could not take that chance, so the ideal solution would be a smaller-scale place of learning, with less students to cavort with.

The day of her medical appointment arrived, and she attended with her aunty Doris in tow. Becca had rehearsed her script thoroughly and would play on the psychological effect of having a misshapen nose. A nurse came out of the doctor's room and called out her name.

"Rebecca Beacon. This way please."

Her aunty Doris got up, but Becca told her to stay where she was and wait.

"I'm OK. I've got it all worked out."

"Are you sure?"

"Absolutely. It's better I go in on my own. But thanks, Aunty Doris, for caring."

Doris shook her head with disbelief and admiration. *She's one on her own all right.*

The surgeon was sat behind his desk. He looked up at Becca and told her to take a seat.

Take it where? she was tempted to ask out loud. She needed him on her side, so any sarcastic remarks were decidedly put on ice.

"Yes, young lady. Your GP has written to me about your problems. Let's examine this for you."

He looked inside her nose with a light and felt around the bridge. After further investigations he walked back to his seat and sat at his desk.

"You've got a deviated septum and that's what's causing the problem. We can straighten the cartilage and that will hopefully help you breathe better."

"What about the bone?"

"What about the bone?"

"Can you alter that into a better shape?"

"I don't think we need to go that far. It's easier just to work on the cartilage."

Becca's dramatic flair came to the fore.

"But Doctor, you don't understand! I want a normal profile! I'm so aware of the bump that I walk about covering my nose with my hand if a bus passes me! I hate it! It's spoiling my life! The other day someone called me Ringo! That was the cream on the cake! Please help me! It's holding me back! How will I ever meet anyone with this trombone hooter? I'm so upset!" she pleaded with a tearful expression. *I should have gone to drama school. Great performance Becca.*

"It's not that bad cosmetically but if it's affecting you to such a large degree, we will try our best to put it right. Now, you're very fortunate because I've just had a cancellation, so we can admit you in two weeks. Are you sure you want such invasive surgery?"

"Positive." She sniffed loudly.

"Right, well you'll receive a letter for admission in the post. If this is getting in the way of your life and confidence, then we will do our best to restore it for you. I have to say that personally, I can't see anything really wrong with the bridge, apart from a little bump, but we will repair it."

After going through the whole operational procedure with her, the surgeon walked her to the door and wished her well. She bit her lip, smiled tearfully and thanked him profusely.

Her aunty Doris had heard her wailing through the wall. "Becca Beacon, you deserve an Oscar for that performance. All that was missing was the audience!"

"I know. How good was I? It did the trick though. One new nose, here I come. Hurrah!"

Becca had her operation in the middle of March. Although she had been prewarned about the surgery, she did not fully realise that it would be so painful. When they wheeled her into the ward after the procedure, she felt as if she'd been hit by a truck. Plaster of Paris was across her forehead and down her nose. Her nostrils were tightly plugged to stem the bleeding and both her eyes were extremely swollen and black. She had a bad reaction to the anaesthetic and was repeatedly sick.

Her parents came to see her the day after and walked past her bed. They did not recognise her, so she waved to them but felt too unwell to speak.

"Eric! Eric! There she is! Oh, my word! What have they done to her? She looks like she's been in a car crash! Oh, Becca!"

They sat at her bedside and Shirley found it extremely difficult to act normally. She could not understand why Becca had put herself through the wringer in the first place. There was no need to break the bone of her nose and reset it.

"The surgeon told us you'll be in here for ten days," said her father, stroking Becca's hand.

She nodded slightly and moaned.

"Everyone sends their love. Mikey is coming to see you later."

"That's if he knows it's you!" carped her mother.

"Shirley! Stop it! She's had the operation and now she has to recover. That's all there is to it."

Becca smiled weakly at her father, grateful for his understanding.

"Anyway, we've brought you the latest Beatles Monthly and some recent articles about them in the papers. When you feel better you can read them," he added.

"Thanks, Dad," she whispered.

"Jean and Julie from your college are coming to see you later. It's a long way for them to travel so I don't know exactly when they'll arrive. Also, Dave rang. He's driving over at the weekend, and he'll visit you. He wants to know if you need anything," asked Shirley, still inwardly upset at the state of Becca's face.

"Just a new nose," she jested in a weak voice.

"The surgeon said there'll be a lot of swelling, but it will go down. He's very pleased with the result and he's sure you'll be happy with the shape," reassured her father.

Becca smiled. It looked more like a grimace, but it would all be worth it to see the back of the bump and those recurring sinus infections.

While Becca was recovering in the antiseptic sanctity of her hospital bed, she had plenty of time to think about the future. Her intense social life had got in the way of her guitar playing and she had misplaced the joy it afforded her. She made up her mind to do two things when she got home. Number one, she would organise her studies in the new college. Number two, she would definitely buy a guitar of her own, instead of constantly borrowing from other people with similar interests.

She had the strangest dream on her last night on the ward. She saw The Beatles at the top of a mountain slope. Suddenly, John slipped on a grassy rock and fell helplessly into a gaping chasm. Then, one by one, they all stumbled and lost their foothold. She was literally calling out in her sleep because she was awakened by the night nurse who comforted her and gave her a sedative. She drifted back into a restless state and tried to think of the morning and the familiar faces of home.

*

The end of May saw her arrival at the new college with a perfectly straight nose. There was only about six weeks left of that particular term, so she tried to adjust as best as possible. She missed the vastness of the college before and felt like the proverbial little girl lost, as most of the students had already struck up their own friendships.

On Thursday 30th May 1968, The Beatles planned a new LP. They had prebooked Abbey Road Studios right the way through until late July. Armed with a variety of new songs, they were not alone. The Japanese artist Yoko Ono joined them because John had left his wife, Cynthia, and now she was the new love in his life, who never left his side. The others all resented this intrusion because the studio was sacrosanct, and they always worked together without anyone else being present. There was a lot of discord brewing on the horizon.

Becca had very mixed emotions about the whole scenario. On one hand she did not want to judge John for his actions, but on the other she felt it was shoddy, especially where Cynthia and his son Julian were concerned.

I'm not judgemental, but he's obsessed with Yoko and the others see her as an interloper. This doesn't bode well for the future. She's really way out, but then so is John. It looks like they connect on a mental level. It's something that was lacking in his life, I guess.

I always thought Paul supplied that for him in their songs and very close friendship. Much more than a rapport really. Two halves that fit together so well, laced with a deep love. Always catching each other's eyes. A very tactile twosome. A bond that goes back years.

I know that things change and can't stay the way they are forever, but I pray that there'll be a peaceful solution to this new situation. The last thing I want is acrimony. I'll just fall apart if it ends badly. I hope that I'm barking up the wrong tree, but I can see the writing on the wall.

*

In June 1968 she met Rob Barrie, her husband-to-be, although if someone had told her that at the time she would have laughed in their face. The furthest thing from her seventeen-year-old mind was marriage. He had asked her out for a coffee a few times, but she'd declined because she was still seeing Dave. Then, one day, she bumped into him at the corner of her street, and he was insistent. Her heart was beating fast because she felt very drawn to him. He had a look of John, but was taller, standing just over six feet. He was manly, rather than boyish, with a presence. In the end she could not resist his allure.

She needed the money to buy her own guitar, so she took a summer job at a local biscuit works, packing their assorted boxes on an assembly line together with other students. It was the most boring task and she felt sorry for the people who had a permanent position there. The hours were long and laborious, starting at 8.30am and finishing at 5.00pm. The entrance was like something out of a concrete jungle. Cockroaches lined the stone steps, eager to enter and have a feast.

One day she borrowed Mikey's guitar and took it into work to entertain everyone in the lunch hour. For her last song she performed a tuneful rendition of 'In My Life', a much-praised Beatles track from their 'Rubber Soul' LP.

"Hey, Becca, you're good!" said a worker called Stan. "I love your voice. You should audition for *Opportunity Knocks.*"

However, the supervisor was not as enthusiastic. She told Becca off, especially when the 'concert' ran over by five minutes.

"You know, you're getting paid to pack biscuits, not to entertain the workers. So, get back in line! You're on the chocolate digestives today, so make sure you don't drop any on the floor!"

"Oh, crumbs. So sorry in advance," mocked Becca.

"You know, if you worked here permanently, I'd get you dismissed!" she berated.

"If I worked here permanently, I'd want you to!"

"Such cheek! Get on with it!" she carped and walked away in a huff.

"Take no notice of her, Becca," said a student called Carl. "She's so uptight."

"Oh, I know her type. I had five years of rules at school. She's a brassy version of my headmistress."

"Would you like a lift home tonight? My dad's doing me a favour. We could drop you off," suggested Carl, with a wide smile.

"Thanks for the offer but my… my boyfriend is calling for me."

Becca's heart flipped when she thought of Rob. He was picking her up with a friend of his, and then later on they would be going to The Midland Hotel for dinner. She had been seeing him on a regular basis and was hooked. *How am I going to tell Dave? He'll be so upset but I've fallen for Rob and want to be with him all the time. Oh heck. I really don't want to hurt Dave. He's been so good to me but what can I do?*

Rob had just turned twenty-one. He was very self-assured and on their first date he'd told Becca in no uncertain terms what he thought of the way she dressed.

"You know, you don't have to wear such a short skirt. It's like a pelmet. Also, your eye make-up is too heavy. You've got lovely hair but insist on wearing it scraped back into a ponytail. It should be more natural," he'd criticised.

"Why don't you say it like it is? I mean don't hold back."

"I'm only telling you for your own good."

"If you don't like the way I look, why take me out?" she'd snapped.

"Because I can see beyond the mask. And I love what's underneath."

"What mask?"

"The defensive wall that you've built around yourself, laced with sarcasm. There's no need for it. You're the sexiest girl I've ever clapped eyes on. And I want you. For myself."

"Oh, well. That makes it all OK, doesn't it?" she'd mocked.

"Look, Becca. I know it's early days, but I've fallen for you. You're different and I really like that. I just want to bring the best out in you. That's all," he'd smiled appealingly.

"You know I'm still seeing my boyfriend, Dave. We've been together for nearly two years. In all that time, he's never found fault with me."

"I'm not finding fault. I'm advising you. As for Dave, well, finish it. It's me or him."

Becca had been really annoyed but gave Rob's words a lot of thought. Once she'd calmed down, she realised that he'd meant well. He was a hairdresser and had his own sense of style. However, she did not want anyone controlling her. She wasn't too sure about another date but when he phoned her to arrange one, she melted. There was something really special about him.

"Hi. Fancy going to the pictures tonight?" he asked casually.

"What do you want me to wear?" she ridiculed.

"Whatever suits you."

"You've changed your mind then?"

"Becca, I've had a long day at work. I just want to be with you. I think about you all the time."

His reply threw her off-balance. It was the same for her. He was in her head constantly.

"What's on?" she asked distractedly.

"On?"

"Yes, at the cinema. What film were you thinking of going to see?"

"*Rosemary's Baby.* It's just up your street. Supernatural and thought-provoking."

"Sounds good."

"I'll pick you up at seven. Afterwards we'll go for a meal."

She agreed and put down the phone as her mother came into the hall.

"Was that Dave?" asked Shirley.

"Erm… no. Mum, I need to talk to you. Have you got a minute?"

Becca told her mother all about Rob and asked for her advice, although she knew deep down that she was going to end up with him.

"Be very sure, Becca, because you're going to break Dave's heart. He thinks the world of you."

"I know, Mum. But I feel more for Rob in two weeks than I've ever done for Dave in two years."

"Well then, you don't need me to tell you what to do. You're still far too young to settle down anyway. Live your life to the full. Time flies. I blinked and fifty years flew by. I just want you to be happy. That's what matters."

"Thanks, Mum. There's just two important things to tell Rob. He doesn't realise the extent of my obsession with The Beatles and musical aspirations. It's vital that he understands."

"Then tell him. He needs to know what he's taking on. It could very well put him off! You're hard to handle. I love you but it's a fact. Mood swings and the bloody Beatles! God help him!"

She spent most of the summer holidays in Rob's attentive company. The hardest part had been finishing with Dave. He had looked so upset when she told him it was over. Becca felt really bad about it, but she could not go on deceiving him. Even worse, Dave gave her the option of going back with him, if she found she'd make a mistake, but Becca had an innate feeling that would never happen.

On the 17th July an animated film, 'Yellow Submarine', was released, featuring The Beatles songs. It was funny to see them as cartoons. Their voices were impersonated, but Becca loved it.

By the end of the summer, Rob was very much acquainted with Becca's poems, sketches, parodies, guitar playing, singing, tantrums and her beloved Beatles. He was very patient considering that none of his past girlfriends had awards for exhibitionism. It took him a while to understand why she functioned in such a temperamental manner. She was prone to low moods which needed support and understanding. And Rob had those qualities in spades.

She had never told a soul about 'uncle' Ted. Even now, it was still transpiring. He would seek her out and stop her in the street to show her pornographic magazines and tell her filthy stories about his sexual fantasies with her. No matter how many times she would berate him, he still persisted in touching or grabbing her wherever he could. He had his hand in his pocket and would play with himself as he spoke to her. It took Becca all her time not to throw up on the spot.

On her next date with Rob, she suddenly decided to tell him about all the abuse she had suffered from the age of nine. Rob wore glasses, but she saw his eyes darken behind the lenses.

"I don't know what to do, Rob. I can't take it anymore. It's left a huge scar and I'm so disturbed."

"Oh, I know what to do. I know exactly what to do," he said through very tight lips.

"I don't want my parents to know. My mum and his wife are so close. It would cause such an upset and I couldn't cope with it."

"It won't come to that. I'll just confront him. That will be the end of it. Believe me."

Rob was true to his word because after that, 'uncle' Ted never even looked at her.

"What did you say to him? He's avoiding me like the plague. What did you do?"

"You don't want to know. No more questions now. He'll never bother you again."

"Oh, Rob. You're so good to me. I'm so sorry for my crazy moods. Truly sorry."

"Nothing to forgive. Now come here and give me a kiss. I love you, Becca Beacon."

"And I love you too, Rob Barrie. With all my heart and boots."

*

Becca's handmade acoustic guitar stood in the corner of her bedroom and looked conceited. She loved its tone and felt it was worth every minute of her summer dead-end job, and the money she had saved packing those assorted biscuits. Now she did not have to borrow anyone else's. Rob loved to hear her play and sing, and urged her to take it seriously.

On the 28th July 1968, The Beatles had what they called 'a mad day out' being photographed and filmed in seven key locations around London, even though they were in the middle of recording their next album. It was to be a collage of fashionable photographs for their fans, something a bit different than the shots of the past. Becca read about it in her latest Beatles Monthly magazine. She noted that they had grown their hair even longer, especially John and George. Yoko Ono was there, along with Francie Schwartz, Paul's new girlfriend, plus the camera crew.

Yoko seems to go everywhere with John now. It's like they're joined at the hip. I get the feeling that the group are all on shaky ground, even though the photos look cool and contemporary.

On the 26th August 1968, The Beatles released their eighteenth single 'Hey Jude', coupled with 'Revolution'. Becca was obsessed once more with their creativity and changing fashion. When it shot to number one, they gave a televised performance on *The David Frost Show*. Becca did not recognise John for the moment. Out of all of them he seemed to have altered the most. It was not just his hair or clothes, but an aura that shone around him. He seemed as magnetic as ever, but with a new blatancy. She soon realised that Yoko Ono had a lot to do with this alteration.

When she read that John was divorcing Cynthia, she did not want to question it. It really was not anyone's business but being victims of continual publicity, it was easy to spread the news. As Yoko became more and more a part of The Beatles scene, Becca sensed a growing resentment within the group itself. When John was ridiculed for his choice of partner, Becca would spring to his defence, but really it was only John's protection and welfare she cared about.

She went back to look at the latest contemporary photographs from their 'mad day out'. She pushed away any negative vibes and just admired the pictures of them. She was still besotted with John and Paul, and everyone knew it. Even Rob was getting sick and tired of her endless admiration and thought that she should concentrate on her own endeavours.

"Hey Rob, just look at these pics. I can't get enough of the Fabs. They keep churning out their amazing songs. It's never-ending. I adore their creativity. They really inspire me on many levels."

"Well, if they inspire you to such an obsessive degree, why don't you write your own songs? You've been telling me that's the aim. So, go for it. I want to hear about you. Not just them!"

"I've always wanted to do that but I'm holding back for some reason. I think it's because I won't live up to my icons."

"Even your icons had to start somewhere. I've got faith in you. I know you can do it."

"Do you really think so?"

"I just said so. I love to hear you sing and play. Make your own music, Becca. It's time."

Becca was inspired that Rob had urged her to take her music more seriously, and in September 1968 she wrote her very first song. She was babysitting for some friends with Lynne, who was reading a book. The house was full of character, a bit like its owners, who were both musicians.

She picked up an acoustic guitar that was in the room and began to play. Her imagination was working overtime and as she strummed, she began to create a melody in her mind. The tune reminded her of an emptiness, a sadness, a lament. She imagined an estranged lover sat in a field of flowery profusion and visualised the hollow melancholy she was feeling. She scribbled down some lyrics and folded them in with the melody. And that was it. Her first self-penned creation.

She snatched the paperback out of Lynne's hands and grabbed her full attention. Lynne jumped with the suddenness of Becca's actions.

"Lynne! Listen to this! It's called 'Wondering.'"

"What is?"

"My song. I've just written a song! I can't believe it."

Lynne looked at her as if she'd flipped her lid as she listened to a repetitive performance of Becca's first original creation.

"What do you think?"

"I think you're crazy, but I like it. It's simple but haunting."

Maybe to Lynne it was a moment of madness, but to Becca it was the beginning of something spiritually rewarding. It was the first step towards the creative life she had always craved. It was the start of something indescribable and the very foundation of her future song writing abilities. She could not wait to play it to Rob. She was seeing him tomorrow and looked forward to his opinion.

When she got home, she played it on her own guitar to The Beatles gallery on her bedroom walls, and could have sworn she saw a complimentary nodding of their four prolific heads.

*

Her second term at college arrived. Without realising it, her work showed a marked improvement. It was only a small building and students received individual attention, which was a virtual impossibility in a larger place of learning like her previous college. She made a few friends and felt a lot more contented than she had anticipated.

She was seeing Rob regularly and spent a lot of her spare time improving her song writing. She bought a reel-to-reel tape recorder and made quite a few recordings in his house at the weekends. By now she had written another four songs. Rob particularly liked one called 'River Blues'.

"You're holding back a bit with your vocals," he advised. "Let yourself go, you've got the power in your voice, so use it."

"Do you like the songs though?" she asked, always needing his encouragement and approval.

"I think you can do even better. They're improving all the time. Instead of writing about imagined situations, why don't you put your own feelings and experiences into your songs? That way, you can express your true self through the music and lyrics. You can do it, Becca. I know you can. Not being able to read music isn't a drawback for you. You've proved that."

"You're right. I was just experimenting but now I'm further along and can create melodies. The lyrics are a doddle. I've always loved words. But the music just comes into my head from out of the air. I just strum along, and the melody seems to wrap itself around the chords. Having a good memory helps, otherwise I could easily forget the tune. But once I've created it, then it remains forever in my mind. So, yes, it's time to express everything I've always wanted to, in a song."

"That's my girl. The sky's the limit. Let's carry on, and later we will make a different kind of music. Won't we?" he said suggestively, and Becca's heart skipped a beat.

"Yes, Mr. Barrie. Whatever you say."

He blew her a kiss and they carried on recording. Rob took all of these sessions seriously and wanted to bring out the best in her. She felt inspired by his faith in her abilities.

By now she only knew a handful of people who admired The Beatles. Even then, it was not with half of the feeling she still had for them. She would inadvertently bump into lost faces from school who looked at her sideways if she mentioned her icons in conversation. Obviously there were plenty of fanatics still hovering around, but she did not encounter them anymore.

Only yesterday I spoke about their changing creativity and appearances to an acquaintance from my old college. She gave me a glance as if to say, "haven't you grown out of that childish stage yet?" How could she possibly understand that because of my own gift for song writing, I'm drawing nearer than ever to the band? How could they really grasp the meaning of my one-time unattainable dream that's now floating steadily towards a tangible destiny?

On the 22nd November, The Beatles released their ninth studio LP on the Apple label. It was a double album, and the cover was just plain white with the name of the band embossed on the front. It featured thirty songs in all and was always going to be known as the White Album. It had been a long time in the making but when Becca listened to the eclectic mix of compositions, she could understand why.

Firstly, she was bowled over by the diversity of melodies. Secondly, she had multiple rows with so-called fans who thought that it was all completely over the top, with no direction or continuity. Thirdly, she railed against the critics for pulling the album to pieces because they thought it was disjointed, hackneyed and pretentious.

"Diversity is versatility!" she raved to Rob. "The reviewers must be stark raving mad! Have *they* ever written a song in their life? I bet *they* couldn't write the bloody alphabet with a dictionary in front of them! They make me puke!"

"Calm down. It's not worth you getting so worked up."

"Calm down? Calm down! It's an injustice! The Beatles are pure genius. Fucking critics!"

"Becca! If you don't shut up, I'm going home! Quite honestly, I'm getting sick and tired of your obsession. Enough!"

She stopped raving when she saw Rob's angry expression.

"I can't help it. They're my world. Apart from you."

Rob shook his head and walked out, leaving Becca in a state of high anxiety. *Now I've gone and done it. Oh heck. I'll go round and apologise. He just melts when I hug him. That'll do the trick. Bugger.*

Just before Christmas 1968 she gave a concert at the college party. She had added quite a few more songs to her repertoire and it went down exceptionally well. Even the lecturers admired her gift.

During the holidays, she visited many people and places with Rob. All the time she felt that it would not be long before some kind of irreversible altercation would occur within The Beatles' group. There was too much pressure, too many hangers-on, too many differences of opinion, too many songs written individually by the four of them. Firm management was desperately needed. Not a parasitic entourage. Not the presence and influence that Yoko Ono had over John. He seemed permanently aggressive and cynical towards everyone. Brian Epstein had left a massive hole, and the oneness they all shared seemed fragmented and fragile. Becca felt an intuitive uneasiness. She knew deep down what it meant. It was the creeping rot that would effectuate the death of The Beatles as a band, and something in Becca would die from the dissolution.

Chapter Ten

The beginning of 1969 saw Becca in the college good books. The results of her half-yearly exams showed great promise. She thought that the praise received was rather undeserved. Her mind hardly ever circled around her secretarial future as much as her theatrical aspirations. She gave a lot of credit to her lecturers, who had the ingenious knack of capturing her interest and attention without methods of repression.

Becca was rarely enthusiastic about her college course, despite the good results or comments. As the time for her departure into the outside world drew closer, she would break out into hot sweats of apprehension. The only thing that kept her placid was her musical aspirations. And it was because of this inner anxiety that she really discovered the true release of song writing.

On the 30th January 1969, The Beatles performed and filmed a spur-of-the-moment concert on the roof of their

Apple Corps Headquarters in London. The keyboardist, Billy Preston, joined forces with them as the band played a live, forty-two-minute set of five of their songs. The noise reverberated around the city and the police arrived, ordering them to turn down the volume.

Apparently, the event had been envisaged only a few days before and they had been planning to return to live performances since they had started recording sessions for their future LP, 'Let It Be'. However, it was to be the very final public performance of their whole career together. Crowds of spectators, many on their lunchtime break, gathered in the streets to listen. Others accessed the rooftops of nearby buildings to hear some of the unreleased songs. The concert ended with 'Get Back' and John in his typical zany way said, "I'd like to say thank you on behalf of the group and ourselves, and I hope we've passed the audition."

Becca saw a report on the television news that same night. Her heart sang at the sight and sound of her beloved Beatles, playing and singing together again.

"Rob. I never thought this would happen. I've had genuine psychic feelings of them splitting up. I hope I'm wrong. They seem completely in tune with each other."

"Well stop being so negative," he replied.

"I'll try."

"Anyway, I've got some good news for you. I've managed to wangle you a spot at the Free Trade Hall. It's a charity event and you'll be on the bill. What do you say to that?"

"The Free Trade Hall? Oh, my goodness. It's huge! We had our Speech Days there when I was at grammar school.

It's the home of the Halle Orchestra. Do they know that it's just me and my guitar? I've no backing group. It's just me on a stool."

"I'm sure they'll get you a stool. It's not a problem."

"I know that! But I'll be singing original songs. What if they don't like them?"

"Just throw in a few Bobby Dylan numbers. Becca, this is a great opportunity."

"I'm nervous, Rob. I want to do it, but I don't know if I'm good enough."

"You're more than good enough, Becca. You're ready for this. I wouldn't let you do it if I thought you weren't. You have a talent for song writing and a voice to go with it. People need to hear you."

"Oh, heck. OK. Yes, I'll do it. But you have to be there at my side."

"Where else would I be?" he replied, putting a protective arm around her shoulder.

Becca chose five songs to perform. Three were her own, one was Bob Dylan's, and the other was Leonard Cohen's. She rehearsed in her bedroom, looking at her Beatle-decorated walls. *I can do it, John. I know you'd want me to, Paul. It's exciting and nerve-racking. But Rob's right. People do need to hear my songs. I'm improving all the time. The melodies are more tuneful, and the lyrics reflect my mood. So, the Free Trade Hall, here I come!*

Becca would never forget the first terrifying moments before her act. It was a big challenge because she had never played to such a large audience before. Her opening number was 'Love Minus Zero No Limit', a Dylan song, and she was petrified that she would forget the words.

It went down well, so she gave a first rendition of three original songs and prayed inwardly they would make an impression. Then she sang Leonard Cohen's 'Dress Rehearsal Rag', also a very lyrical song.

The audience's reaction was really enthusiastic. She did not know why she was received so kindly, because she felt her guitar playing was not up to scratch. But it left her with a deep desire to perform from that day onwards.

"Rob, I feel so high! They liked me! I'm so happy," she gushed.

"See. I told you. It's just the start. There'll be much more to come," he replied confidently.

"Yes, please! I just love it! It's where I belong. By your side and on the stage. How good is that? Wahey!"

*

Paul married Linda Eastman on the 12th March 1969. Then John married Yoko Ono eight days later on the 20th March, in Gibraltar. The Beatles nineteenth single 'Get Back' was released on the 11th April, backed by 'Don't Let Me Down'. Becca contemplated as she revelled in the two new songs. The flip side was appropriate. *Don't let me down, Johnny and Pauly. Stay together. Please!*

All four Beatles had developed other interests and formed new relationships outside of the group The newly formed Apple Corps company dealt with their own marketing and merchandising. However, after a year of overspending, Apple was to employ a new manager to sort out their complicated finances. Paul wanted his father-in-law to take over, but the other three Beatles signed a three-year contract with Alan Klein. It caused an even deeper rift.

John started The Plastic Ono Band with Yoko and several other musicians. On the day of their wedding, they staged what they called their first 'Bed-In' for peace. Their second 'Bed-In' was held in Montreal in late May and early June, where they recorded 'Give Peace A Chance'. It was the first single released by John outside of The Beatles.

There were newspaper articles hinting at the acrimony and ill-feeling John felt against his fellow Beatles for not accepting Yoko, or indeed, respecting her. There was also much speculation about the possibility of the band breaking up. Becca felt unsettled to say the least.

Oh, God. I wish I'd never clapped eyes on all of them. Oh heck, I sound like my mother now! I didn't really mean that. It's just so horrible. Why have they got to destroy all the joy they brought to the world. What's going on?

They've grown apart. I know that they're older and have different lives, but why can't they be civil to each other?

It wouldn't be so hard if it was just a peaceful parting of the waves. At least the glorious memories would be intact. It's taken the shine off my own creations. I don't know why it means so much to me. But it does.

*

The Beatles released 'The Ballad of John and Yoko' with the B-side 'Old Brown Shoe' on the 30th May. Becca liked the sentiment because, regardless of her reservations about Yoko, she felt that John had the entitlement to marry the woman of his choice.

The last day at college was meant to be celebratory. Becca had passed her exams and gained distinctions in all of them. She went to a nearby tavern with a host of friends, her guitar slung over her shoulder. The juke box was kept alive every minute they were there, and Becca kept choosing Beatle songs. Everyone was laughing at her loyalty towards John. Most of the kids loathed his long-haired appearance and ideas, and especially the strange bride beside him. Becca was angry over their insults but the more she boiled over, the harder they laughed. It was not John she was defending, but what he represented. The right to placard a belief no matter how off-beat the plan. The right to voice his opinion without being ridiculed. The right to stand tall.

"Oh, come on, Becca. He's lost the plot. What's all that Bed-In rubbish about? There are better ways of advocating peace. And she's worse! What do they expect to achieve?" mocked a student.

"I don't care about how it looks. I don't really get it myself. It doesn't matter how avant-garde the method is. What really matters is the message. 'Give Peace A Chance' is an anthem for change. What's wrong with that? What's right with war?"

"What's right with them? They're a joke."

"Well laugh all you want, but I'm telling you this: anyone in my book who advocates peace and love is more philanthropic than those mealy-mouthed politicians spouting lies."

"You're just defending him because he's a Beatle."

"No, I'm not! This goes beyond his Beatle status! He's found his true self. I wish with all my heart that he could have attained this with Paul, George and Ringo. But I can see it's not to be. It kills me that their bond is broken. Because it is, you know."

"You don't know that for sure."

"Oh, but I do. I've felt it coming for years. I didn't know exactly the way it would happen, but I could read John's face and get inside his head through his songs."

"Aw, Becca. Never mind him. Let's hear some of *your* songs. It's our last day together."

"In a minute. I'm just going to the loo," she lied.

Instead, she sat on a chair in another part of the pub. They had rubbed her up the wrong way and she tried to put her thoughts in order. It hit her hard that she was thinking of John as a separate entity, as a being in his own right. She conjured up a mental vision of The Beatles, but he did not seem to belong with them anymore. She had always respected his status as an individual, even within the group's framework. She found it sad to think of him outside that melodious forcefield.

When she was ready, she went back to her friends. She picked up her guitar and sang her heart out to expel all the emotion she was feeling about John. She had actually written a very contemporary song about him, called 'It's All In The Mind.' The melody was haunting and the lyrics were very applicable:

Nobody knows of the thoughts that arise from his tortured mind
He is the one who is breaking his head trying to reach mankind
Ooh – what lies within?

A naked reflection of one who is trying to win
Ooh – flashes of light
Blinding his eyes and his brain as he tackles his worthy plight.
Clamber along some invisible thread of eternity
Think of the time you have spent thinking why should you feel so free
People – well they laugh at your hair
Laugh at your clothes and your theories they don't seem to care, at all
Ooh – you fool on the hill
Drown in the sweet scent, remain there 'til you've had your fill
You wonder if ever the day will arise when you'll leave the clan
And feed them with knowledge, the wisdom now you are that other man
Ooh – you think it's a sin
Flick back your hair with a motion that's helped along by the wind
Ooh, you stand by the light
Feel incredibly high as you dance by the side of the moths in the night

The tears began to flow down Becca's cheeks from the emotion she felt. There was a stunned silence and then a deafening applause. Her friends gathered round her in a show of heartfelt solidarity.

"Oh, Becca. That was so amazing. You really do love John Lennon," said Rhona, the student who had mocked him initially. "It doesn't matter what I think, does it? You deserve a cut of his royalties for your loyalty."

"All I want for John is happiness. It breaks my heart in two that it's not with the group. You can't even begin to know what they mean to me. Or what they did for me. I will always love them."

"Is Rob picking you up? He's such a lovely looking guy. So tall and self-assured. He's got a look of John, you know. Is that why you've fallen for him? Is it, Becca Beacon?" Rhona laughed, trying to lighten the mood.

"Well, it helps," joked Becca.

"Seriously?"

"I love Rob with all my heart and boots. He's beautiful inside and out. That's why I get how John feels. When you find your soulmate, you instinctively know. I think Rob and I will be together a long time. I'm nineteen in September. He's spoken about getting engaged for my birthday."

"Really! Wow, Becca! That's great!"

"I'm thinking about it. It's a bit too soon. Maybe next year."

"What's to think? All you need is love. You've sang that often enough to us all. So, grab it and grab him."

"I might just do that. Now let's put another Beatle record on the jukebox."

*

Towards the end of June, she visited quite a few office bureaus for interviews. Her exam results were excellent, and she knew there would be no problem in landing a job sooner or later. As she was assessed, she felt more nervous than if she was playing to a capacity crowd of thousands.

For the first time, she was embarking on a stage of financial independence. This should have been a pivotal moment, but she did not like the idea of a routine existence.

In July she was ready to earn her first week's wages. The office was very modern and the staff friendly enough. Ironically, the building was situated near Granada TV Studios, so she only had to look out of the window to see the glorious sight of that structure.

She would receive countless flashbacks to the summer of 1963. She pictured her twelve-year-old self on a Raleigh bicycle, and the many hours spent hovering around with her friends, all of them living in hope that The Beatles might be visiting the location. She also remembered with clarity when she wagged school in 1965 and 'broke in' past Albert, the commissionaire, on the day they had filmed the Lennon and McCartney special.

Becca was working solidly away but was extremely tired, because on the 21st July 1969, at 3.56am British time, the American astronaut Neil Armstrong had emerged as the first person to walk on the moon. He strode out of the Apollo 11 Lunar module and onto the moon's periphery, inside a sector termed The Sea of Tranquillity. Rob was very much into science fiction and had read every book on the subject. He was utterly fascinated by outer space from a non-fictional and fictional viewpoint. He was literally over the moon about the whole achievement. It was an amazing moment and they had both watched the incredible footage on television, so they had no sleep that night. He made it even more interesting for her by his vast astronomical knowledge. But then again, he made everything thought-provoking because he was so well read.

The next day she had travelled into work, her head still full of lunar landings. Her job seemed even more mundane, but she concentrated on the pile of correspondence that her boss had dictated. She sighed deeply because she was already feeling sleepy, bored and disinterested. She had only been working for a few weeks when a cloud descended on her and never left from that day onwards. She could not relax with a nine-to-five existence, and it gave birth to a plethora of songs. She expressed her disillusionment in the music and lyrics. It was an ideal release, and her creations took a turn for the better.

All her doubts about the end result of her college education loomed before her in an alarming reality. It pinned her down. She was effectively a prisoner of her own making. The more trapped she felt, the greater the urge to create. In her lunchtimes, she often typed out her feelings on office paper, sketching endless images of John and Paul and using the photostat machine to make copies.

"Why are you still working, Becca?" asked the big boss. "It's lunchtime. Go and get yourself something to eat."

"Oh, I'm fine. I've bought some sandwiches with me. I've just made a cuppa to go with them."

"Well, I'll say one thing for you, you're very keen!"

"Well, I like to do my best. They taught me that at college. I've always been a stickler for the rules," she lied magnificently because she did not want him to see her concoctions.

"If the youth of today were all like you, the world would be a better place," he praised.

Becca smiled widely. *If only you knew.*

"Anyway, I want to dictate some letters around two o'clock and there's also a very important report that must be submitted today. Sharpen your pencil because I need your excellent shorthand skills to complete all these tasks. It's quite comprehensive but I'm sure that you'll cope admirably."

Becca carried on with her writing. She was really frustrated and had to put down her thoughts.

And I'm sat here. So, what now? Is the traffic moving because I'm still? So many unanswered questions. When I think about the different people around me, are they moving? No more queries now because the mood is passing. There's just the usual feeling of segregation.

And on the office wall is a picture of a nude for the purpose of advertising petrol. And life is rather bizarre when it wants to be. Still the telephone rings. I can't be bothered to answer it. And still the thing lives.

How can I be what I was yesterday when tomorrow never comes? What is the meaning of it all? Perhaps a childhood memory, my yellow swing, or a cloud in the sky. So I am, as I am. And I know what I know. Is this the precious climax to it all?

*

On the 29th August 1969, Becca and Rob, together with friends Lynne and Gary, decided on the spur of the moment to drive down to The Isle of Wight Festival at Wootton Creek. Bob Dylan was headlining along with The Who, Free, Joe Cocker and quite a long list of acts. Becca & Co headed for Portsmouth, where they would link up with a ferry that carried vehicles on board.

It took over five hours to get to the harbour, but they were all up for it and eager to soak up the whole atmosphere. Even though 150,000 people were expected over the weekend, that did not stop them wanting to be there. However, they did not go prepared, and ended up sleeping overnight in the field along with thousands of hippies.

Becca could not switch off because she knew that John, George and Ringo would be present, along with Keith Richards from The Rolling Stones and Eric Clapton. There was little chance of seeing them in such a crowd, but just knowing they were there was enough.

There were food stalls, but they were ridiculously expensive, and not too hygienic, so they ended up eating cold baked beans and bananas. The toilets were portable but permanently in use and the queues were long. Becca and Lynne found a patch of land that was amazingly unoccupied, covered in shrubs and bushes.

"I need a wee and I don't want to wait. In fact, I can't wait," said Becca, desperate to go.

"I'm the same. Let's go in that field over there," suggested Lynne.

Becca pulled a face but really did not have a choice *I'll have to crouch down pretty low just in case there's a psychedelic 'uncle' Ted lurking near the foliage.*

Becca sat on her heels in a rather undignified pose, only to feel the most unbearable shooting pain up her backside.

"Ow! Ow! Lynne! I'm on a bunch of stinging nettles! My bum's on fire!"

Lynne burst into hysterical laughter. "Stop it, Becca. I'm going to wet myself."

“Well just be careful where you plonk down,” she moaned, repositioning herself in a safer spot.

Lynne had a fit of the giggles and could not stop. She remembered Becca’s torn trousers at The Beatles concert in 1965.

“What is it about you and your bum? Torn hipsters and now thorny bushes. Oh, Becca, you crack me up. Out of all the spots you had to find that one! You’re a scream!”

“Some joke! It’s already itching and red. I won’t enjoy anything now. Bummer! Literally!”

Lynne laughed even louder. “We’ll have to see if they sell any ointment or natural soothing products.”

“Oh, the stalls are just brimming over with nettle-sting remedies. I mean they’ve got a plentiful supply of ‘up your bum’ emollient. It’s the deal of the day.”

“You never know. Just ask. Becca, you’re a one-off.”

“So I’ve been told a thousand times. Ouch! Talk about ‘Ring of Fire’ by Johnny Cash!”

They made their way back to Rob and Gary where the whole place was littered with youth. Becca felt lost in the crowd again. Regardless of the musical ambience, she still felt isolated from all those hippies, who seemed to have cut-glass accents and walked around with an air of false wonder.

She sat down cross-legged on a make-shift pillow of Rob’s padded jacket and felt no sense of belonging. She really did not function with any of those flower children. Neither did she fit in with the go-getters of the office brigade. So where was she relevant? There was only one answer. She nestled between the mind-crunching layers of her musical creations, where she shone.

She knew by now that her revered Beatles were dying, that the strain of mismanagement would result in a bitter parting of the waves, and that the business wolves were waiting to rip the heart out of that commercial empire. And she knew they would succeed. It seemed that as she hit upon her own creative salvation, her icons were in the process of obliteration.

Regardless of her whirling thoughts, she enjoyed the music at the festival and wished she was one of the acts on stage. *Maybe one day I will be. Who knows?*

Bob Dylan was the main reason they had travelled all the way to the Isle of Wight. Becca was trying hard to stay awake after a sleepless night, and to her absolute dismay she fell asleep through the bulk of his spot. She was so annoyed with herself, but then her highly developed sense of the ridiculous kicked in and she saw the bizarre side of it all.

We've driven miles to watch Dylan perform. So what do I do? Drift off into the land of nod. I'm awake for every other act but zonked out for the main attraction.

Those canned beans have given me chronic wind and I'm trying hard not to trump on a continual basis. My bum's still in nettle-shock and I've got two blackheads on my chin. My clothes feel manky, and I look like something three cats have dragged in.

Apart from that it's all hunky dory. Ah well, such is life. Mine's outlandish, singular and unique. Thank fuck for that!

*

On the 26th September 1969, a few days before her nineteenth birthday, The Beatles released their LP 'Abbey

Road'. It was the last one to be recorded but not the final album to be issued. They had been making a film of 'Let It Be' with songs to go with that particular project, but the actual footage took so long to shoot that the LP was held back to correspond with the movie release.

The front cover of 'Abbey Road' showed them walking across a zebra crossing. Paul was the only one in bare feet, and the conspiracy theorists had a fictional field-day out over the fact. Rumours had been circulating that Paul had died in 1966 and had been replaced by a lookalike. They even went so far as to claim that John sang the words "I buried Paul" in the fade-out of 'Strawberry Fields Forever'. So, the barefooted Paul was now absolute 'proof' of their conjecture.

That's right, and I bet they hid the body in his guitar case! And I thought I had a vivid imagination! This lot puts me firmly in the shade. Blockheads!

Around this time, Rob had booked her into a recording studio to get down four of her most recent original songs. It was just an acoustic session with guitar and voice. Becca double-tracked her voice in parts, and also harmonised with herself. She took to the whole experience like a duck to melodic water. The song titles were 'Echoes of The Laughter', 'Painting the Past', 'Japanese Girl' and 'It's All In The Mind'. When it was finished and played back to her, she sounded tuneful and confident. The engineer had done justice in capturing her true vocal range.

Rob ordered three vinyl discs of the recording in an EP format, specifically two songs on either side. It all came out of his pocket and was quite costly for something that might just lie around. It needed a professional hearing for an opinion.

Becca need not have worried, because Rob had other ideas now that he had something accomplished in his possession. He visited the house of a friend of his, whose daughter worked as a secretary for the owner of Rare Records in Manchester town centre. She listened to the disc and liked it a lot. She then said she would try and raise some interest within her company. Her persistence triumphed because they were called to see the owner to discuss a possible publishing contract with his associates in the music business.

"I really think you've got something here," he said to Becca in his office. "I'd like to manage you. I've got major contacts at the Ditchburn Organisation, whose label is Domino Records. Have you written any other songs?"

"About twenty or so," she said, her heart thumping in her chest with excitement.

"Have you brought them with?"

"Er, no. They're on tape."

Rob noticed an acoustic guitar in the corner. "She can play for you, if you don't mind her using that guitar," he suggested, pointing towards the wall.

"Good idea. Is that OK with you, Becca?"

"Erm… yeah. Have you got a capo so I can change the key? I don't do bar chords yet."

"Yes. We sell them downstairs. I'll ask my assistant to bring one up. By the way, call me Irving."

"Call me Beatle girl."

"Beatle girl? Do you like The Beatles then, Becca?"

"No. I don't like them. I adore them."

"They're splitting up by the looks of it," affirmed Irving. "I get all the inside news through my contacts. It's a pretty heavy scene."

"I know. Please don't talk about it."

"Becca, play Irving your latest song. The one you sang for me last night," interjected Rob, moving rapidly away from the subject of The Beatles when he saw Becca's sad expression.

"You mean 'Star'?"

"That's the one."

Irving's assistant came into the room at that very moment with a steel capo. She clamped it on to the neck of the guitar, which shortened the length of the strings and raised the pitch into the key she desired. She cleared her throat, sat on a chair and launched into her newest composition. Like so many of her creations, it was very contemporary and lyrical.

And you stand on your hill, see the many lucky people
The many lucky people walking down below
And you think to yourself, are you something like those people
Something like the people walking down below
Then you sit on the ground and you take in all around you
And though no-one hasn't found you, you don't wonder why
There's a star in your eyes and it's shining rather brightly
And you know it has the right to be up in the sky
And you stand on your hill 'til the night is all around you
And its beauty just astounds you while you're standing there
And the star seems to glow as it shines along your pathway
And the wind makes its journey through your moonshine hair
So you sit on the ground and you take in all around you
And though no-one hasn't found you, you don't wonder why

There's a star in your eyes that is shining rather brightly
And you know it has the right to be up in the sky
Yes you know it has the right to be up in the sky.

Rob, Irving and his assistant all clapped. Becca felt ten feet tall and still growing.

"Did you like it, Irving? Be honest with me."

"Honestly? I think you're an undiscovered talent and I want to do my best to get you on the road to success. Your song writing shows promise and I'd love to hear you with a band. I'm going to call my friend Jim, who owns Domino Records. Just leave it with me. I'll be in touch soon."

Becca was feeling very excited about the whole development. She could hardly concentrate on her work, which was becoming more and more tedious due to the progress in her musical career. She would carry out her duties like an efficient automaton, using any spare moments to type out her poems, observations or song lyrics. It was a good job her boss could not see the amount of photocopying she did behind his back and at his expense. The work left her cold and empty, but she really abhorred the evening rush hour. Everyone would be pushing and shoving along with selfish preference, almost as if there was in imminent alien invasion. She was never a lover of crowded places and the tumultuous five o'clock ritual moved her to screaming point.

She had forgotten the number of times she boarded the train home in a state of intense melancholy. Other people seemed to adapt much more willingly. She would push her discontentment and frustration along the railway track and let it lie in some derelict siding until the morning light. A lot of the headache had a great deal to do with the job itself. The people and surroundings were pleasant, but the whole pantomime was not Becca. And that is exactly what it meant to her. A pantomime in a winter, spring, summer or autumn production.

Her mind was too full of music, always working out new ideas for songs, forever analysing situations and thoughts. In the end, her office environment appeared like a watered-down version of school life, with a pay packet instead of batch of homework. The same sort of people were in control. The same manipulation prevailed. The same characters were fencing her in. Anyway, they could not have possibly understood the conflicts that battled away inside her head.

As 1969 drew to a close, she pondered upon the arrival of a new decade and what it would bring. She knew it meant the end of the rough, tough and tender moments of her teenage roundabout. It would herald a new generation of youth and a different musical scene. She hoped that some kind of headway would be made with her music. She hoped that her and Rob would go from strength to strength. She hoped that her fears of The Beatles break-up were all unfounded, or that a potential parting of the waves would not be acrimonious.

As the clock struck midnight and she said goodbye to the tumultuous 1960s, she shed a tear. A tear that symbolised the happy sadness of the past ten years. A tear that trickled unashamedly down the cheeks of a frustrated shorthand typist who no longer wished to hide between the folds of The Beatles' creations, but who desired strongly to gain her own musical recognition.

The chair is high, the swing is low
The world is one huge puppet show
The fences loom before my eyes
In ardent, eager, shrewd surprise
The traps, the trials have set their time
I'm walking on their railway line
There's no path back, I'm here to stay
No little children in my way
I'm on the road to revolution
So how come there's this institution
And who are you to tell me when
The lion's crouching in his den.

Epilogue

It was 1970, and a cold, crisp January day. Becca was playing The Beatles single 'Something' and it's flip side 'Come Together.' It had actually been released last year, on the 31st October 1969, and it was the first time that George had written the A-side. She knew that John and Paul wrote separately now. The eyeball-to-eyeball creations were a thing of the past.

"How come you're not playing the mopheads' songs as much?" asked her mother. "Not that I'm complaining. You're usually fixated on their LPs. You only seem to listen occasionally now."

"It's not that I don't want to, but I'm spending a lot of my spare time writing my own stuff. Make no mistake about it, Mum, I still love them with all my heart and boots. It's complicated."

"You're complicated!"

"Well, you had me."

"And I wouldn't change you for the world. Even though you drive me mad with your crazy ways. Changing the subject, have you and Rob set a date for your engagement yet?"

"Not an exact one but we're looking at June. That's the month we met two years ago."

"Well, do keep your father and I in the picture. We'll have an at home celebration party. I'm so glad he's here for you, Becca. You're an independent girl but you function far better with him at your side. You're feisty but vulnerable. It's a strange mixture, but that's the way it is."

"I guess."

"Right. So, what's happening today?"

"Well, I'm going to sign a management and publishing contract. I can't believe it, Mum. It's so surreal."

"Not really. You're very gifted and you deserve it, even though your Beatles have been the main inspiration. I suppose I have to thank them for that. So, some good has come out of my suffering."

"Oh, Mum. You like a few of their songs. Come on, admit it. Dad was whistling 'Yesterday' before and you were humming the tune."

"It's a one-off."

"Like me?"

They hugged. Then Becca got ready upstairs for her special day, all the while kissing her latest Beatles posters that were still dominating her bedroom walls. *Wish me luck. I'm on the way.*

By now Becca's songs had improved greatly. Her publishing contract spurred her on. She performed at a variety of venues, including university circuits and concert halls. She would dedicate whole weekends to composing. Rob was behind her all the time, pushing and coaxing. She felt that other people thought it was just a phase. In the past she had been so indecisive about her life, so they found it hard to believe that she was actually serious about something.

Her parents totally understood and encouraged her greatly. *Mum was gifted musically with her amazing vocal range, and Dad played piano and banjo. He's also good at art and paints pictures. They never really had an opportunity to pursue their talents due to the times they were born in. If I achieve recognition, I will be their second chance because they would look upon my success as their own.*

Becca marvelled at the way her life was turning out. Her Beatles affinity had proved beneficial. All through the years she had listened to their music, loving and worshipping their creative abilities. And now, here she was doing the same thing, embarking on a career that could bring similar rewards. Making her own music. She knew all along that they had entered her life for a purpose, or else the magic would have rubbed off long ago. With these thoughts in mind, she managed to tackle her everyday working life, but always rushed home for a musical release.

*

March arrived with sweeping winds, stealing April showers without repentance. Becca received a call from her manager informing her that he had booked a session at Strawberry Recording Studios in Stockport next month to get down all her latest material, and also to introduce her to the head of Domino records. A possible recording contract was in the offing, and she felt the excitement running through her veins.

The week before that initial meeting was spent with Rob, practicing the songs she would perform and record. He was very stimulated by the news and fussed around her like a child with a new toy. They asked a mutual friend who played accordion if he would accompany Becca on one of her numbers that had a French feel to it. The song was called 'Sign of Love' and had a beautiful melody that was very appealing and quite continental.

The session was a total success. Domino records liked what they heard, and a recording manager came into the picture. An agent was found, and a future single was discussed. It all happened so quickly that Becca thought she was going to fall over. The atmosphere at home was tingling with expectation, but amongst this frenzy Becca's life was abruptly shattered.

On Friday 10th April 1970, Paul gave an interview to publicise his solo album 'McCartney' and told the world that he had left The Beatles. Unbelievable to the many thousands who had ignored the warning signs, but not inconceivable to Becca. It was totally expected. *Oh, God, it's happened. It's true!*

And what a way it happened. It was hostile. It was bitter. It was venomous. It was vile. It was pure poison. It was the strain of many factors and grievances exploding in a million pieces, with claws of vengeance. They were critical of each other as insults flew around like dispersed sycamores.

Becca stood alone, as rigid as a marble statue. She had foreseen it and yet she could not believe it. She could not work out why she felt so broken. It was not as if she had ever really known them. But it was as if a part of her had died. She felt so sad, and the tears began to fall.

The dream was over.

*

As the year progressed along with her career, she read so many versions of why her icons had parted company and was sick to death of the different explanations. She could have spat at the sensation-seeking journalists who kept reminding her of that painful day in musical history.

She loathed the way that John and Paul attacked each other, and the articles of indifference. She abhorred the whole nauseating legal drama of their bitter separation. She even hated John for saying that The Beatles were just another band. She wanted to inform him that because of his 'band', she had found her inner self. She needed to tell him that she was never a part of the 'hype' or 'portable Rome' of his frustrating years as a Beatle. She yearned to let him know that she never expected him to stay forever within the same musical framework. She wanted to congratulate him, and Paul, and George, and Ringo, for their continual sparkle of individual creation. But more than anything, she longed to erase all the enmity and acrimony.

She knew what John meant by The Beatles 'myth'. She knew they were never the innocent mopheads of their manufactured image in those early years. But their close bond saw them through it all. She respected their reasons for the new ventures they wanted to pursue. She always knew that their success had made them prisoners of their fame. She knew they were never perfect. Who is?

Crucially, without their contagious influence, would she have ever discovered her own identity? Where would she be now? Without her music?

When the first signs of creative awareness spewed forth in an alarming urgency, revealing the very roots of her innovative energies, destroying all conception of daily continuity, and trying to converge with the brilliance of her contemporaries, it was as if she was reborn. She watched, listened and learnt. Was it solely because of them? No. It was *always* inside her, lurking and waiting to blossom but needing that special catalyst. They did not make it, they just found it, replenished it, smoothed it and cultured it. So how could Becca think of them as 'just another band'?

How could she forget the fact that she grew up alongside their own hectic lifestyles? How could she dismiss the absolute joy and pleasure they afforded her through their incredible music? So, how could she ever accept the venomous way that they shed their famous cloaks of recognition and shovelled dirt on every part of that once intrepid team? It was not the split. It was the manner. Nothing lasts forever. She had made a mistake in believing in their projected infallibility.

It was hard for an outsider looking in. It was hard for her to take it in all at once. It was hard to rely on newspaper talk or colour television for any true conclusions. It was an ending that was perhaps as predictable as its beginning. The invisible scissors dissecting the Chelsea boot and the jelly babies, destroying the Liver Buildings and the Mersey dockside.

All I know is that I was once a twelve-year-old imp with a profound desire to see them. And then I grew taller, and the infatuation materialised into deep admiration for their songs. But they have served their purpose and opened the door for so many artists of today and yet to come. Including myself. God bless The Beatles! Their influence will never die.

*

On the 8th May 1970, their delayed LP 'Let It Be' was finally released. Her hands trembled as she put the vinyl disc on her turntable. She loved it. Of course. How could she not? A collection of their final swansongs, still sounding fresh and unique regardless of their divorce.

In June, her parents threw a glorious party to celebrate Becca's engagement to Rob. The house was full of guests and the food and drink was flowing.

"Hey Becca, play us a song!" requested her brother Mikey, who had qualified as a teacher and now taught art in a secondary modern school in Leeds.

"Which one? You choose."

"Any of them, as long as it's your own."

She grinned widely and picked up her faithful guitar. Her father told everyone to be quiet.

"Our Becca's going to sing one of her own songs called 'Road of Destiny'. It's being recorded as a single soon at Strawberry Studios in Stockport with professional musicians," he enthused.

"Dad! They don't need to know that yet. It's still in the making."

"So what? Let the world know!"

"The world is a huge place. Isn't it, Becca?" said her aunty Doris lovingly, quoting the words she used when Becca told her all those years ago about her feeling that The Beatles were going to conquer every country, and Doris had doubted her prediction.

"I was right though, wasn't I, Aunty Doris? About The Beatles, I mean."

"Yes. You were right. And I was right all along about you. I knew you were special, Becca. And now we all know."

"Well, it took her a bloody long time to get to grips with reality," interjected her aunty Doreen. "She's still got her head in the clouds, but now her feet are also on the ground. Such a strange combination. And I'll tell you what, I'm so glad those bloody Beatles have split up!"

"Aunty Doreen, nothing I do will ever meet with your approval, but I still love your ginger cake."

Everyone laughed as Becca sat on a chair with her guitar and played her forthcoming single. Rob looked at her with love and pride as she began to sing.

I've travelled the road of destiny
I've had a hard but sheltered life
In my book of my life's history
There's a record of joy and strife
Though I've conquered the fields
And I've mastered the sky
And I've talked to the rain and sun

I've never had time to share my world
'Cos I'm always on the run
In a forest of pine and spruce my friend
I have sat cross-legged on the ground
And I've swallowed the sunset in the sky
And the dewy scent all around
And I've reached out with trembling hands so small
To caress the cool night air
I'm away on my lonely, silent cloud
That nobody else can share
Golden clouds smile down on me
And they smile for only me
In my forest home I am never lonely
When the morning comes I stretch my arms
To greet the day once more
And I head for the road of destiny
'Til I reach it's shining door
With guitar on my back and sun in my hand
I can face the world with pride
And I skip down that endless golden road
With freedom on my side
With freedom on my mind.

Everyone clapped enthusiastically and Becca felt ten feet tall.

"What a beautiful melody, Becca. It must have taken you some time to compose it. And you played without a music sheet," said her aunty Mary.

"I can't read or write music. It just happens."

"How? It's not possible."

"Oh, but it is, Aunty Mary. I pluck it out of the air and around a chord sequence of sorts. It just comes to me.

Once it's complete, I remember the tune."

"It's a gift. It has to be a gift."

"It is."

"What about the lyrics? They blend so well with the music."

"Words are my true expression. I've always written, even as a small child. Once I have the melody then the words just flow."

"Well, I wish you all the best, Becca. You have the talent, so go for it!"

"Go for what?" asked Rob, as he popped up out of nowhere, putting his ever-protective arm around her shoulder.

"My career in music. Aunty Mary is just telling me how much she likes my song."

"It's only the beginning," he smiled widely.

"And more importantly, it's our beginning," she said lovingly, and kissed him on the mouth.

*

Becca had another of her vivid dreams that same night. It was very surreal. She was with The Beatles in a large room, but she did not know where it was. She did not realise that she was dreaming and saw it as a chance to tell them all about herself and what they meant to her.

"You made America an easy gateway for British artists. Before you went out there it was very difficult to conquer the music scene," she said earnestly to Paul.

"It wasn't easy in the end. We had a lot of pressure. All that stuff with the Ku Klux Klan was pretty heavy."

"I know that, Paul. And I was very worried about the situation for you all."

"Not as much as we were," mocked John.

"Wanna bet? I was petrified for you when I found out about it all. Don't underestimate my fear by proxy!"

"What's your name? Do I know you? I feel that I know you! Where are you from?" questioned John with a frown.

"From your eternal fanbase, and I don't agree with you when you said The Beatles were just another band. No way! That's the understatement of the century. And my name's Becca Beacon."

"Cheeky little bugger, aren't you?" he commented with a wry smile.

"So I've been told. My mother blames you."

"Me?"

"Yes. She thinks we're hatched out of the same rebellious egg."

"Is she right, Beatle girl?"

"Spot on."

"Well then, welcome to my incubator, Becca Beacon."

"Why are you all at each other's throats?"

"The reports make it worse than it is. But it's still not good," commented George.

"Can't you settle it between you amicably? I mean, keep the legalities to a minimum? But more than that, be kind to each other," she pleaded.

"Don't look at me, I'm just the drummer," scowled Ringo.

"You've influenced me to write songs. I wouldn't have a career in music without you."

"What type of songs, Becca? Nursery rhymes?" mocked John again.

"Well, that's a childish reply for a kick off."

"Cocky as well. Did you learn that at school?"

"I hated school, and the teachers hated me."

"So that's another thing we've got in common. I think your mother's right."

"I've loved you all since I was twelve years old. That may not mean much to you now, but it meant the world to me. I was abused as a child by my mother's best friend's husband, and it went on for years. My therapy was your music. I would have had a breakdown without you. I'd lose myself in your songs. Over and over and over again. For nearly eight years. You are so much more than just another band. So much more!"

The four of them looked at each other and were speechless.

"And another thing, John. You're constantly banging on about peace and love. So, love each other again, why don't you? Practice what you preach. It's achievable."

The four of them looked at her intensely as Becca continued her lecture.

"Your influence carries on in my music. As it will with many other artists. So, no matter what you all achieve as individuals, don't ever underestimate the sheer joy and happiness you brought to the world as a whole. Yes, it became unbearable at times, and I totally get that, but your music will live on. It will never die. And that's the legacy that you will leave. In a hundred years' time, The Beatles will still be around. In one way or another. Generation after generation. Especially with me. Here and now. In 1970. A new decade."

"Beatles and Beacons, huh?" said John, with a twinkle in his eye and Becca's heart sang.

She wanted to hug him, but she woke up before she could.

It was the strangest dream she had ever had, and it left her feeling euphoric even though nothing was really achieved. But she did get to tell them everything she had always wanted to. Albeit in a vision.

*

In the morning she felt inspired to write her conclusions down about her icons. She knew it would be the last time she would refer to them, as her own career would take precedence. So she felt obliged to do so. She began to sum up the whole scenario. Just for posterity.

The Beatles have served their purpose and they have had their time. They have unlocked the door for so many artists of today and tomorrow. They have opened up the floodgates in America for British artists with something to offer. Before their invasion it was very difficult to conquer the music scene out there. They have revolutionised the whole music industry and left a creative scar upon every country.

They continue to influence many of today's writers. They have stimulated the writing of numerous books and articles about their timeless supremacy. They have incited the cynics and delighted the admirers. They have given substance to the poets and created paintwork for the artist's pallet. They will remain a legend. A legend that will live on as long as music exists. Their songs will be remembered and played for centuries to come.

The hysterical reaction to their live appearances will be remembered by an adult generation who were once fans in their frantic audiences. Who could have possibly foreseen the stupendous impact they achieved? Who could have predicted the astounding success of four young men from Liverpool, who hardly had a penny to their names, and ploughed their way through a strength-sapping apprenticeship and rejection.

Did they ever realise the chaos and hysterical disruption they were going to effect? Only in their dreams might they have imagined the staggering heights they eventually achieved. Dreams that materialised into an exciting but frightening reality, a reality that often appeared like a dream world. A world that was bordering on insanity. A world that owned and fed them on idolatry and persecution. A world that never wanted them to leave its spinning rotation because of its own selfish needs. Because the world needed to carry on dreaming.

My reason for loathing their departure is simple. It's not childish and it's not selfish. I always knew that the time to say goodbye would come, but I wanted it to be a clean break. No regrets. No shortcomings. That's all. I just hated the way it was done.

But that's how it happened, and it seems a great pity because when they had nothing, they had everything. And when they had plenty, they died. Still, the world will not let them rest in peace.

No matter what happens with my own career, I owe them everything. I will always be grateful to them for showing me a pathway, for bringing out an ability for song writing that may have taken years to discover. But most of all, for helping me find my true self.

Not only will they live forever in my wonderland of castles and sunshine, but they will hold a place of rejuvenation in my soul and will be remembered and exalted as the most incomparable influence I will every encounter for the rest of my life. Be they four, or one in four, their music will go on.

So, to all you control freaks, and those people who had no belief in my work, read this.

My stormy past is vaguely known
The wind has set its course and blown
All doubting reason from my mind
And put me on the trail to find.
I seek, I weep, but want to know
The answer why the wind should blow
For this would surely make me see
The error of uncertainty
So who are you to show me how
This gifted actress takes her bow.

About the Author

Fran Raya lives in Manchester. Her career has been predominantly in music as a singer-songwriter, and she has performed throughout Europe – notably as the support act for Eric Clapton on his Scandinavian tours in the 1980's. Presently, she concentrates on songwriting only, and pitches her songs to other artists.

She is a member of The Guild of International Songwriters and Composers (GISC) and has been featured on the front page of their quarterly magazine, together with a comprehensive biography inside the periodical.

Her poetry has been published in numerous anthologies and as a result she was awarded her own book, Thoughts of the Poet.

She has also had a series of six supernatural thrillers published with The Book Guild.